J. Lyric Smith Presents:

Running Through Glass Doors: The Loving Family

Volume I

Published internationally by J. Lyric Smith:
PO Box 942253, Atlanta, Georgia 31141
runningthroughglassdoors@gmail.com

A Prelude to Love:

As sure as the sun rises in the east and sets in the west, there will always be this thing called love. Even in the midst of war and times of havoc, there will be some young man loving some young woman or some old woman loving some old man.

Love is a foreign language that needs to be taught and nurtured. Love needs no translation or interpretation. Love is an emotion, an action, a reaction, and a state of being. Love has the power to heal and to wound. Love can create peace and incite war.

Some find love in the church; others find love in the club or even on an app. Some search all over and never find love even when it has always been right in front of them. Love is a locked box that opens with the turn of the right key. Love is a feeling, and you will know it when it finds you, or you find it. Love regulates your heartbeat, changing its pattern when it's near. Love is like a cycle of air that flows through the nose, which fills up the lungs and is exhaled out of the mouth. Love oxygenates, love captivates, love guides.

Truth be told, love means different things to different people. Before you read this fictional tale, you should ask yourself; what does love or being loved mean to you? If you don't have a clear answer, don't worry because you may just identify with one of the characters and their relationship with love. Open up your heart to experience the Loving Family and their relationships, struggles, and triumphs with this phenomenon called love.

Love is the stage, and they are the actors playing their prescribed roles in this juicy topsy-turvy tale of love gains and losses. They are the Loving's, and this is their story of "Running Through Glass Doors."

Chapter 1:

Gaining Control of Love, Uncle Brennan's Pool

June 6, 1990

"Kalila, I bet you can't hold your breath longer than me," yelled Ren.

"Uh huh, yes I can. I can hold my breath so long you gon' think I'm a goldfish," Kalila yelled in her squeaky voice!

As Ren shook his head he said, "I bet you won't make it past the count of twenty."

As the only girl and the youngest in the house, Kalila was always up for a challenge. She took one last look around her uncle's lavish built in pool, held her nose, inhaled the deepest breath she could, and submerged her head into the cold clear blue water.

Ren started counting to twenty. "One, two, three, four, five, six, seven, eight."

With each passing number, Kalila felt more and more free. It felt like every weight was lifted off of her, she felt buoyant. She felt free as a helium balloon being set free from its anchor. Underwater, she felt in control. Abstaining from air was her way of gaining control. If she lived or died, it was only up to her. Kalila loved that feeling. Oxygen deprived she made the conscious decision that she would not let anyone control her decisions or her ever again. She fell in love with this new found feeling of control and flirting with this thing called death.

As a nine-year-old black girl in the nineties coming up for air was one of the only things that she had under her control, and she refused to relinquish it. Her father, Darrell Loving controlled her every move. It was like he feared that if he didn't, she would end up like her mother, Darlene. Kalila's mother had the most control over her, and it pained her that she would never live up to the unrealistic expectations that were placed on her.

The silence under the water was deafening. She was all alone listening to a melodic concert of her thoughts. She felt the cool sensations of her pigtails swaying with the waves of the water, and the wind blowing against the nape of her neck. The water coddled her. Kalila felt as free as a baby fish that separated itself from the school. The last thing she remembered was her brother Ren reaching the number fifty-five, and yelling for their Uncle Brennan and brother Davis.

Most children believed that they were invincible. While submerged under water, she thought about the reality that with life, there was also death. Kalila had dealt with death before, but until that very moment, she never thought of the possibility of death for her.

Oxygen deprived, Kalila started hallucinating; she saw her lifeless body in a pink casket floating in the water right beside her in the pool. Long stemmed white roses surrounded the casket. The thought of her lying dead in a coffin didn't make her sad, it actually made her feel a sense of relief. She felt a profound and eerie connection to death. As the water began to fill her lungs it was becoming all too real for her; as much as she wanted to stay underwater, a primal instinct caused her to start to fight for her life. The freedom and control that she felt underwater were succumbed by the primal instinct to thrive. It was at that moment that Kalila's love affair with death began.

Her Uncle Bree pulled her out of the water and resuscitated her, and it has been his air that has kept her going ever since that day at the pool. I know what you are thinking, what did a little girl have going on in her life that would make her even start to contemplate her demise? Kalila felt as if she was doomed from the start.

Kalila, Davis and Ren spent every summer at their Uncle Bree's house. They waited all year to spend the few weeks of summer break with him. Brennan, or Uncle Bree as they called him, never had kids of his own, so he spoiled them. Their Uncle Bree was rich, at least that is what Kalila and her brothers Davis and Ren thought. He gave them things that their parents couldn't afford to. Uncle Bree made sure that they had what other kids their age had. He bought them their first bikes, school clothes, shoes, and even paid for them to go to a private Catholic school. Those gifts made their father Darrell feel inadequate and were the cause of many disagreements between him and their Uncle Bree. Darrell knew that they needed help, so he did not stop their uncle from doing for them, but did everything he could to prevent Brennan from going overboard.

Uncle Bree made most of his money by flipping houses. He lived in a gated community on the affluent north side of Baton Rouge, Louisiana. His neighborhood was so nice that you had to enter a code just to get through the front gate. Kalila, Davis and Ren looked forward to pulling up to the front entrance of their uncle's community, and they all took turns sitting on their dad's lap to enter the gate code. Kalila would be the one who would remind her brothers of the code, she never forgot that gate code… zero, one, four, three. Putting in that gate code did more than open the gate to his community, it helped to expand their horizons. It afforded them the opportunity to see what was possible if they worked hard. Spending time with their uncle they saw that it was possible for a black person from a small town to actually make it.

Their uncle did not let all of the fancy things he acquired change him. He always told them to value people, not things. It was apparent that he valued his niece and nephews. Their Uncle Bree still had the same friends, ate at the same hole-in-the-wall soul food places, and even attended church on the Southside, their side of town. Though he did not brag or flaunt all the nice things that he had, he appreciated Kalila and her brothers noticing them. He loved receiving praise.

Brennan enjoyed exposing them to things that he thought they never experienced before. He had the latest and greatest in everything. They were young, but they caught on fast; the more excited or in awe they were, the more he would try to expose them to. They definitely gave him the praise he was looking for. They acted like they were not used to nothing when they were around him, like slaves introduced to the big house for the first time. They oohed and aahed at everything. As the only girl, Kalila felt like a princess in her uncle's castle those few weeks she spent with him every summer.

His house was entirely different from theirs. He had a built-in pool, a hot tub, a fireplace, and even had a housekeeper. Kalila and her brothers lived in a modest shotgun house. When you entered the front door of their house, you could see clear to the back of the house. Only pool that they had was their bathtub on a hot summer's day or one filled with their own tears. Not to mention a maid, but if you asked Kalila, she would say that she was it.

Their family was far from perfect, but what family is? This is the story of their collective truths.

Love has its way of finding control in chaos...

Love is not invincible; if you don't invest in it, it will die like a plant that has gone without water.

Chapter 2:

Preparing For Love

Darlene "Dee" Carr- December 31st, 1968

"Come on Mae, it's time to go! If we don't leave now we gonna be late," Darlene screamed as she pulled up her pantyhose.

"Girl I just have to hot comb the back of my hair, I'll be ready in a minute, stop rushing me, Mae shouted!" Mae placed the hot comb on the eye of the stove, ran a piece of paper towel over it, and then combed it through her hair. The hot comb sizzled as it passed through Mae's coarse cold black hair, and the smell of burning hair filled Darlene's tiny shotgun house.

Mae shouted from the kitchen, "You got any more hair grease?"

"Look in the back of the medicine cabinet," Darlene said.

"Oh I see it," Mae said as she grabbed the jar of Murray's Pomade from the back of the medicine cabinet and continued to hot comb her hair. A couple of minutes passed and she shouted, "shit…. Darlene, Dee, Dee."

"What now Mae, and don't be calling my whole government name," Darlene said in disgust as she left her bedroom and walked toward the kitchen to see what Mae was making all the fuss about. She knew that it had to be something bad because Mae didn't swear.

"I burned my ear girl," squealed Mae as she held her right earlobe.

Darlene examined Mae's ear as if she was a doctor on a burn unit, and prescribed the only remedy that she knew to prescribe, it was her mother's cure for any skin burn. She went inside the icebox and cut a slice of butter.

Darlene gave Mae the slice of butter and said, "put this salve on it so we can go, nobody told you to wait until the last minute to try to press your hair anyway. Girl, there is nothing that is going to stop me from going to this New Year's Eve party!"

Darlene walked back to her bedroom and turned up the volume of the radio that was playing faintly in the background just as the beat dropped from one of her favorite songs. Dee began to sing. "R E S P E CT, find out what it means to me."

"Is that the new Aretha?" Mae shouted from the kitchen.

"Don't worry about who I am listening to! You just worry about finishing your hair so we can get out of this house," Darlene replied.

"You just can't wait to showcase yourself around that party for all the men to see." Mae placed her hands on her voluptuous hips and pranced into Darlene's bedroom walking back and forth imitating Darlene's walk.

"Girl I do not even walk like that. Let me show you how it's done." Darlene stood up straight, placed her hands on her hips and modeled her outfit for Mae. As she walked around the room, she said in her best announcer voice, "Modeling her very own creation we have Darlene Carr. Darlene is one-hundred and twenty pounds, light skin, hazel eyes, with long silky cold black beautiful hair."

Mae interrupted Darlene's announcement, "120 pounds? Girl, you know your skinny self have never seen the scale over one-hundred pounds."

"Girl, I am big-boned. You just jealous." Darlene replied.

They both laughed as Mae slapped Darlene on her backside and said, "let's go with your big boned self."

"Now that I am eighteen, nobody can tell me nothing. I am a grown woman. I can strut my stuff for anyone I want," Darlene exclaimed.

Mae said jokingly, "nobody wants your stuff, with your tiny little self." They both grabbed their things and headed out the door to go to the party.

Darlene Carr

One of Darlene's biggest fears was ending up alone. She had her best friend Mae, but Jimmy was courting her. Even though she was barely eighteen years old, she had experiences beyond her years. The months after her parents died, she had to do things to survive that she would never speak of, but would never forget. Darlene lived without regret, but she hated that others took advantage of her dismal situation.

After her parent's died, she was surrounded by many people, but still felt so alone. Most of her family in Baton Rouge was comprised of money hungry distant relatives, and most of them were jealous of her mom and dad. When her parents fell from grace, they saw it as some type of Karma catching up with them. Darlene lived from pillar to post after the funeral while awaiting the insurance money. Once her family found out that there was no insurance money let alone an inheritance, they packed her up and sent her back alone to her parent's shotgun house. After a few months, Darlene was penniless, alone, and taken advantage of. On her eighteenth birthday, Darlene received an unexpected call from the insurance company informing her that she actually had a small trust fund. That money saved her life.

The only company that Darlene had was the reply of the squeaky wood floors as she walked on them. If she didn't have Mae, she believed that no one else would have cared if she lived or died. While most eighteen-year-olds were preparing for college, or still had their parents planning or controlling their lives, Darlene was doing what she had to do to survive. People are the product of their collective experiences, and those experiences made her the woman that she is today.

Her mom was known for having one of the most beautiful singing voices in their town. Rosaline's Carr voice was as powerful as Mahalia Jackson, and yet at the same time as gentle as Diana Ross of the Supremes. Listening to her mother sing, you knew that there must be a God. She sang around the house while cleaning up, and captivated anyone within earshot of the sound of her melodic tone. She had a gift, and she passed on that gift to Darlene.

Darlene's mom taught her many life lessons. Darlene recalled one day when she came home from school and smelled heaven on earth. She remembered smelling collard greens, cornbread, and fried chicken. Darlene was so excited about the meal that she rushed and completed all of her homework, washed her hands, and sat at the table with anticipation. Her mom asked her,

"You ready to eat baby?" She responded as most nine-year-olds in rural Louisiana would, no matter what the question posed by an adult, "yes ma'am."

Darlene watched as her mother's polka dot dress flowed as she walked to the kitchen cabinet to grab a plate. Darlene heard an orchestra of sounds...pots and pans, spoons tapping excess sauce from them on the side of the cast iron pots and pans, the icebox opening and closing, the eye of the stove igniting, and she sat at the table and eagerly anticipated the meal. Her mother came back to the table, and Darlene's mouth salivated. Her mom then walked passed her with a plate fit for a king headed to the den where Darlene's father Murphy was sitting watching television. Her mother placed the plate in front of her father with a glass of freshly squeezed lemonade. Her mother went back to the kitchen and made Darlene a tuna sandwich, with some red Kool-Aid to wash it down.

That was Darlene's first lesson in love. If you are not the focus of love's attention or intentions, you may be neglected. As time passed, Darlene's mother taught her many more lessons, most were about how to keep a man. She told Darlene that the keys to keeping a man were six simple things:

1. Don't let your man smile in any other woman's face.

2. Don't let no other woman feed your man, the key to a man's heart was through his stomach.

3. Please your man in the bedroom. If he is pleased, you should be too.

4. A man is going to be a man. He may slip up and cheat, but that means you have to work harder to keep him. Don't let that other woman win.

5. Never talk back to your man. No man wants a woman whose flippant.

6. Don't show a man that you are too strong; he will be intimidated and leave or even beat you.

Darlene witnessed as her mother repeatedly neglected her own needs for her father's, and sometimes even hers. Darlene loved her mom dearly, but she was destined not to be the woman she was. She admired her parent's relationship but didn't like the imbalance of power that existed between her mother and father. Darlene understood that her mother did what she knew or was taught to do by her own mother, but she promised herself that she would be the one that was going to break that cycle.

Darlene's mom once told her that she knew from the moment that she laid eyes on her father that she was going to marry him. Darlene's parents were married for over twenty years, and Darlene yearned to find that kind of love. Darlene's father Reverend Murphy Carr served as the pastor of Mt. Zion Church in Baton Rouge, Louisiana for over ten years. If you looked up God-fearing in the dictionary, you would probably see his face. Rev. Carr was so charismatic. Watching him preach from the front row made Darlene's heart flutter. He had a way with words; he could convince you that if you didn't put your last five dollars in the collection plate, you might be going to hell. His sermons convinced, motivated, and rebuked. Darlene believed that most of the women in town didn't come just for the word, they came to church to see her daddy. He was the type of person that no matter what you were talking with him about, just being in his presence made everything feel right.

Her mother and father's love for each other was apparent until the very end. Darlene never understood death opening it unprejudiced doors to greet the two people that embraced good, and embodied love for her. Death came in like a thief in the night and stole them from her. They would not get to see her get married, have kids, or raise a family. Her parents were found dead in their bed holding hands with their chests riddled with gunshots. The court found the church secretary guilty of the heinous crime of passion. Because of the circumstances that surrounded Darlene's parent's death she stopped attending church and lost her church family.

Deep down inside Darlene blamed God for his part in removing her parents. She believed that if God truly loved her, he would not have left her alone to fend for herself. The situation, and a series of unfortunate events that happened after her parents died transformed Darlene from a naïve young lady to an untrusting woman. Darlene promised herself that she would always look out for herself, never let anything come between her and her dreams, and always guard her heart.

> *You have to find love inside yourself. When there is none, you have to believe in something or someone greater than you that can fulfill your expectations of love.*

Chapter 3:

Love Staked Its Claim

Darlene (Dee)- December 31, 1968

As Darlene and Mae entered the VFW hall for the Annual New Year's Eve party, they saw the crowd of people on the dance floor and became even more excited. The ceiling of the small hall was covered with black and gold helium balloons, and the strings attached to them gently brushed against their faces as they approached the middle of the room. There were all classes of people there disguised in their "good clothes." It was hard to distinguish the difference between the bootlegger and the preacher, or the town's whore and the faithful wife. Everyone was dressed to the nines.

The anticipation of the New Year and the fanfare of the event intoxicated each participant. A five-person band filled the room with the sweet sounds of Martha and the Vandellas, Aaron Neville, Four Tops, Ray Charles, Aretha Franklin, and even the Supremes. Eligible and not so eligible black folk came from all over the city to attend this annual event. It was said that if you were searching for love, it could be found there.

As soon as Darlene and Mae heard the baseline of one of their favorite songs, "Heard it through the Grapevine," by Marvin Gaye, they made eye contact and they knew it was time to cut a rug. Darlene and Mae listened to that song so much that they even created a routine to it. Darlene grabbed Mae by the hand and pulled her to the makeshift dance floor that was illuminated by multicolored flashing lights.

Marvin Gaye's voice sent vibrations from Darlene's spine to her "pocketbook." As they danced, Darlene felt a tap on her shoulder. She turned around with an attitude and thought to herself, who in their right mind would have the nerve to interrupt her while she was dancing with her girl. As Darlene turned around, she made eye contact with one of the most good-looking men she had ever laid eyes on. He was six foot three with light brown eyes, caramel skin, and a smile that could sell you sand on a beach. It was as if the music had stopped and they were the only two people in the room. He asked her to dance, and she couldn't help but say yes. As she accepted his offer, he grabbed her by the hand and pulled her close to him, and they two-stepped for the duration of the song.

21

The disk jockey announced, "Up next we will have a live performance of the Temptations' My Girl." The band began to play a slow acoustic version, as a sultry male voice belted, "I got sunshine on a cloudy day." As they danced he wrapped his hands around Darlene's waist, and pulled her closer to him. He smelled so damn good to her. She rested her head on his shoulders, and he softly whispered the song's lyrics along with the performer in her ear. As he sung to her, his lips gently touched her ear. She had to bite her bottom lip to keep from screaming in excitement. Darlene just wanted him to put his lips on every part of her. By what she was feeling below, she wasn't the only one enjoying the dance. She did not want the song to end.

He stared deeply into her eyes as the song ended and asked, "What's your name beautiful?"

For a moment she forgot her own name. After a couple of seconds of gazing into his beautiful brown eyes, she replied, "My name is Darlene, but my friends call me Dee."

"It is truly a pleasure to meet you Dee, I am Brennan, but Folks call me Bree."

They both laughed because their nicknames were so similar and they actually rhymed.

"Are you from here Brennan, I mean Bree?" Dee asked.

"My brother Darrell and I recently moved here from New Orleans. Are you from here?" Brennan asked.

"I am. I have been in Baton Rouge Louisiana all my life, but I have big dreams. So you better get to know me now before I have an entourage of security folk keeping people like you from disturbing me while I am dancing with my girl.

They both laughed.

Dee continued, "Really Bree! This small town is looking smaller and smaller each day."

"Big dreams huh?" Brennan laughed and said sarcastically.

"You will see my name in lights one day, I'm going to be a star," Dee replied in a matter of fact manner.

Deep down inside Dee did not know exactly what she wanted to do to become famous, all she knew was that she wanted to be far-far away from Baton Rouge. She was not truly passionate about any one thing. She could dance, sing, and people always have told her that she had a face that should be on the big screen.

"I am going to be a star," Dee said again as if she was trying to convince herself, and as if Bree did not hear her the first time.

"I would love to see that! I really enjoyed our dance, but I got a confession to make." Bree said as he stopped invading Dee's personal space.

"You don't like women?" Dee asked.

"Nah, it is nothing like that," Bree said as he laughed.

"Then what is it?" Dee said in a matter of fact manner.

Brennan looked down at his dress shoes and said, "My brother Darrell actually asked me to come over and get your number for him, but you were so beautiful I had to get a dance."

"So you came over for your brother?" Dee asked.

"He saw you first, and staked his claim on you," Brennan replied.

"Staked his claim? What am I some type of uninhabited land? Tell your coward ass brother-"

"No, it's not like that Dee," Brennan interjected.

"Like I said, you can tell your coward ass brother that since he wasn't man enough to come tell me he was interested in me, he for damn sure is not man enough for me."

Brennan's eyes made contact with someone standing behind Darlene. Brennan placed his hand on his lips.

"Oh no! You did not just try to shush me."

24

"Dee-" Brennan said.

"He is behind me isn't he?" Dee asked curiously.

A silky deep voice whispered into Darlene's ear. "I couldn't come over to ask the ebony queen to dance myself cause I was on the microphone singing my heart out to her. Did you say your name was Dee?" Darrell asked.

As Dee began to turn around, Darrell gently held her shoulders preventing her from turning to face him. Darrell warned Darlene that once she turned around that her life would never be the same. She slowly turned around, and before their bodies were squared completely, Darrell kissed her on her lips. She slapped the taste out of his mouth. She didn't know where his lips been. But once Darlene looked into Darrell's eyes, it broke her heart to see him hurt. Darlene regretted slapping him, but she didn't apologize. At that moment, she had an unexplainable urge to make sure that Darrell was comfortable, to make him feel better.

Darlene couldn't explain the way she was feeling but knew in her heart of hearts that there was something special about this man. It was more than his looks, but she had to admit that he was a sight for her two eyes. Darrell was cut in all the right places. He was tall dark and handsome with a small well-groomed afro with the cutest gap in-between his teeth. He had dimples that were so prominent that you could sit a penny in them.

"Alright Yawl, it is about that time," the disk jockey yelled as he began the traditional countdown. The crowd enthusiastically joined in, shouting "TEN."

Darrell whispered in Darlene's ear, "There is something special about you Dee."

-NINE

She thought to herself, could this Negro be reading her thoughts. Just in case, she cleared her thoughts by thinking about what she was going to eat when she got back home like there was actually a possibility that he could be reading them.

Then Darrell said, "I will make you happy Dee."

The crowd shouted, "EIGHT, SEVEN, SIX, FIVE, FOUR!"

Darrell continued, "I knew from across the room, that you were the woman who I would spend the rest of my life with."

-"THREE!"

Darlene thought to herself, Negro please, he would say anything to get a nightcap. It was crazy, but a part of her believed him or wanted to. Then Darlene said the first thing that came to her mind, "I bet you tell those lame lines to all the girls."

-The crowd shouted "TWO!"

26

Darrell said, "Shut up and kiss me."

-"ONE!"

They kissed, and it was cosmic. Darlene saw fireworks and felt an implosion of sensations deep inside of her as Darrell's lips pressed against hers. While Darrell was kissing her, she opened her eyes. He was looking straight at her; he never closed his eyes. Later on that night Darrell told Darlene that he did not close his eyes because he feared that he must have been dreaming, and he did not want to wake up from this fairytale. No man had ever made Darlene feel the way that Darrell did in that moment. Darlene will never forget when the clock struck midnight January 1, 1969.

Darrell and Darlene have been inseparable ever since that night at the VFW hall. Some people spend their lives searching for love, but for others, love stakes its claim on them.

> *Real love has no competition; you will know it when your love arrives. When you choose to let love in, make sure it is your choice and not someone else staking their claim on you.*

Chapter 4:

Responsibility for Love

Darlene (Dee) & Mae September 23, 1971

"I am so happy for you and Jimmy," Dee exclaimed.

"What is there to be happy about Dee?" Mae said as she placed her hands on her growing belly.

"What do you mean, what is there to be happy about? You and Jimmy are getting married tomorrow. You guys are meant for each other. Girl, tomorrow you will wake up and be Mrs. Mae Jenkins," Dee said reassuringly.

Dee laid across the queen sized bed in the hotel suite that she booked for Mae's bachelorette party. She looked around the dimly lit room with anticipation, while waiting for the arrival of the rest of the bridal party. Since Mae was too holy to have a real bachelorette party, they decided to have girl's night and give each other manicures and pedicures. If Dee had her way, there would have been strippers, liquor, whips, and handcuffs on the agenda.

Dee stared judgmentally at her best friend Mae from across the room. Who would have thought that the saved, sanctified, and filled with the Holy Ghost Mae would be pregnant before saying I do. Pregnancy did not look good on her either. Mae has always been a voluptuous woman, but pregnancy made her even more voluptuous, teeter-tottering on being fat. Mae never had a sense of fashion, she always beat to the rhythm of her own drum. Looking at and speaking with Mae, Darlene could actually feel her heavy heart. Jimmy and Mae's relationship was filled with drama. One day they were kosher, and the next day they were about to kill each other. Darlene didn't think that Mae ever loved Jimmy or vice versa, but LOVE had its way of making its way inside her.

"Dee, I never expected to be getting married six months pregnant. Do you think he is only marrying me because I am in the family way?" Mae asked.

"Are you serious? You are the complete package chick. If I swung that way I would have been locked you down foxy momma." Dee said as she smacked Mae on her backside and stuck her tongue out at her.

"Mae laughed as she said, " Girl, you always know just what to say. You are my best friend, and I don't know what I would do without you."

To be honest, Dee believed that Mae settled for Jimmy. Jimmy was a low-down shade tree mechanic that chased every vulnerable woman that had car issues. The only form of payment he accepted from most women was something that didn't involve U.S. currency. Darlene expected that Mae would end up with Jimmy or someone like him. Deep inside Dee felt as if she was better than Mae and that Mae was destined for the small town life.

Mae was Dee's best friend, but Dee felt that she had to keep an eye on her. Dee believed that Mae was envious of her. She believed that Mae wanted what she had with Darrell. Darlene knew that it was her fault that Mae was infatuated with Darrell; she gave her too much information about their relationship. Describing in detail how Darrell put it down in and outside of the bedroom and did any and everything to make her happy. Darlene remembered what her mother used to tell her about women; "if a woman was unhappy with her life, she would try to replace her life with yours." Dee took notice of all the compliments Mae gave to her boyfriend Darrell and the way that she was always giggling at everything that he said, if it was funny or not. Dee was glad that Mae was getting married, so when she left the small town she wouldn't have to worry about her as much.

"Mae, I am still mad that you refused to let me throw you a bachelorette party."

"Jimmy would kill me if I did!" Mae exclaimed.

There was a knock on the door. The other two bridesmaids walked into the room, and the ladies began to set up the various nail polishes to start doing their manicures and pedicures. As the ladies were letting their polish dry, they heard another knock at the door. Dee looked surprised as she said, "I wonder who that might be? I got you a stripper," Dee said.

"Please don't tell me you did that Dee," Mae said with conviction.

Darlene walked slowly to the door, turned the doorknob, and the hotel concierge entered the room with a cake that read, "Last Night As A Free Woman."

They all laughed, ate cake, and then went to bed.

Sometimes we are forced into a love for all the wrong reasons. Love is irrational. If you have to rationalize the reason for love, it may not be love.

Chapter 5:

Lifeless Love

Darlene- November 02, 1971

Two months after Mae's wedding, Darlene and Darrell were married. Dee couldn't believe that she was now officially a married woman. She was no longer Darlene Marie Carr, she was now Mrs. Loving. Dee watched her mom and dad do this thing called marriage all of her life, and she thought to herself, "how hard could it be?" She was in for a rude awakening.

The first week of their marriage, Darrell lost his job at the seafood plant. He promised Dee that he would go out and look for another job right away, but that did not happen. Darlene ended up footing all of the bills. Days turned into weeks, weeks turned to months, and almost a year later Darrell still did not have a job. He even stopped inquiring about jobs around town and made the autonomous decision that music would be his career.

Darrell even asked Dee for a small loan from her trust fund to buy instruments for the band he was putting together. Dee gave him the money because she was tired of seeing him moping around the house. From the first day she met him she felt the need to fix him, but who be the one that would fix her? She was as broken as a mirror that fell from a mantel.

The only thing that was good about their relationship was the sex. Darrell was good in the sack, and he knew it. After one night with him, you would have married him too. He was so passionate, and pleasing her was his main objective. His soft kisses on both of her lips and his gentle nibbles all over her body made Dee forget about all of his shortcomings. Only if they could have made love twenty-four hours of the day, they would be the perfect couple.

While Darlene was deep in thought, someone started to pound on the screen door. She heard someone yelling, but she couldn't make out what they were saying. She walked to the front door to see who it was, and it was Mary Lee Harper, Mae's neighbor.

"Dee, you got to get down to the hospital baby!" Mary Lee shouted through the screen door.

"Did something happen to my husband?" Dee asked.

"No," Mary Lee replied"

"Then who?" Dee asked.

Mary Lee, in her hoarse voice, shouted, "It's Mae, she done gone in labor!"

"Where is her husband? Where is Jimmy?" Dee asked.

"I don't know, but it doesn't look good Dee!" Mary Lee shouted.

Dee sensed that something wasn't right, so she ran to the kitchen to turn off her greens, grabbed her keys, and ran out the door. On her way to the hospital, she said a quick prayer for Mae. Darlene wasn't the most religious person, but her parents raised her to believe that in the midst of the storm he (God) can and will provide peace. After her quick prayer, a sense of peace overtook her. She knew deep down inside that prayer truly changed things.

When Darlene arrived at the hospital, Mae was laying in the bed, still pregnant. Darlene felt relieved and thanked God for his grace.

"Hey Mae, how you feeling?" Darlene said with concern.

"I'm okay, I lost a lot of blood. The doctors say that I did not miscarry," Mae said in a monotone fashion.

"Why you look so sad then Mae, that is great news?" Dee said as she sat on the edge of Mae's hospital bed,

34

she hadn't been inside of a hospital since her parents died. Dee was not prepared for what Mae was going to say next.

"My baby is dead inside me. I have to carry this dead baby inside me until I can have it naturally." Mae paused for a second to gather her thoughts, and with a voice as shaky as an out of tune violin said, "Jimmy and I were fussing, and things got out of control, he didn't mean to push me. I was punching him in his face, and he pushed me off of him. That's when I fell down." Like a rainy day, tears started to stream down Mae's face, as she placed her head inside the palms of her hands.

Darlene pulled Mae close to her and told her that everything would be okay. Mae was now left empty because the only love that she ever knew died inside of her.

Love doesn't hurt.

Chapter 6:

Reflecting on Love

Mae - December 21, 1971

It was Christmas time, and the whole world was celebrating the birth of Christ, but Mae was mourning the death of her baby. Mae lost the love of her life. She would never forget the words that Dr. Maynard told her, "You will never have a child of your own." Mae thought to herself, "They took my womanhood... they took my insides." Mae had lost the best thing that she felt that could've ever happen to her, which was becoming a mother. Until she found out that she was pregnant, she thought that her life had no purpose; that baby was going to be her purpose. Mae did not have big dreams of living in the city like Darlene, she was happy to live and die in her small town.

Jimmy found a way in a millisecond to take away her hope, her purpose, and her love. Jimmy did not want her to have anything, and she felt that deep inside he wanted her to lose her love. He wanted her to feel the loss of the only thing she held so dear. The only person that would have loved her for her. Before Jimmy, no man showed Mae any real attention, well the attention that she wanted. Many men only wanted her for her body. She has always been a shapely woman. She began wearing a bra at the age of seven. When she was nine years old, grown men would even approach her and make inappropriate comments towards her. She thought that she was a woman because of all that attention. The attention that Mae received even made her own mother jealous at times.

She couldn't remember one man in her life that didn't molest, harass, beat or rape her. She began to accept the fact that all men were going to do those things to her. She thought that Jimmy was different. She thought that he was the first man that didn't see her as this five-foot-nine voluptuous woman, built like a Coca-Cola bottle. He listened to her. He was interested in her. Interested in what she wanted to do, and where she saw herself.

With all of his good, Jimmy was a jealous man. The same voluptuous body that he was attracted to made him furious when other men would look at it. This was the cause of many of their fights. He monitored everything that she wore. She wore loose-fitting clothes to disguise her full-figure because of all of his insecurities. He chased all of her friends away. The only friend who stuck around amidst all of their ups-and-downs was Darlene. The only reason Jimmy didn't mind her, was because he loved gawking at her. The both of them would joke about how fat she was, and how she needed to eat less and exercise more. Mae was the punch line to every joke when they all were together.

Darlene has been one of Mae's best friends, but sometimes Mae thought that Dee secretly hated her. Mae felt that Dee was just killing time with her. Mae believed that if an opportunity arose, Dee would leave her where she stood. Sometimes from the corner of her eyes, Mae could see Dee looking at her in disgust. Dee and Mae could be going out to a party together, Dee always made Mae show her what she was wearing in advance so that presumably they could match each other. Somehow Dee's outfit would never match Mae's, and Dee's outfit would end up being more lavish. Dee had to be the center of everyone's universe. Mae really believed that Dee thought that life wouldn't go on without her. Mae believed that she was a good friend to Dee, and she prayed that deep inside Dee thought of her as the same. Mae felt that Dee saw her as the reflection of someone that she did not want to be; the person that she was running away from, the face of disappointment.

Mae left Jimmy after she delivered her stillborn daughter Nidra, who name meant sleep. The experience made Mae realize that she didn't need a man to be happy, not if he was going to beat her. She just wished that he would have… as if interrupting her own thoughts she began to wrap her hands around herself hugging herself as if she was a baby being swaddled by its mother. She began to sing the words to the hymn, "Silent Night."

> *Silent Night*
> *Holy Night*
> *All is calm*
> *All is bright*
> *Round yon virgin*
> *Mother and child*
> *Holy infant so tender and mild*

As she fought back her tears, she finished the stanza.

> *Slee-eep in heavenly peace*

Tears began to roll down her eyes, as she proclaimed, "my dear Nidra, my love sleep, sleep in heaven until I join you when I leave this place. Sleep my love, Sleep, my love."

> *No matter how much time passes, the loss of love still hurts. That hurt won't be overcome until it is replaced with a new construct.*

Chapter 7:

Love Sowed

Darlene(Dee) & Darrell-March 1978

Trust fund balance, seven dollars and fifty-two cents. Darlene and Darrell ran through all the money that her parents left her, mainly because they were just taking from it and not contributing. Because of their current financial situation, Darlene had to find a job to make ends meet. When there was an opening at Midnight's, a nightclub downtown she jumped on it. It's crazy right, who would have thought Darlene would be singing full-time as a featured performer. Her mom would have been so proud of her. Darrell was finally working too. He also performed at the club; his band went on right after Dee to close out the club. After watching Darrell perform night after night, she began to see why he fought so hard to do what he really loved to do, music. Music was his first love. She knew from the moment that she first heard him sing at the VFW hall that his love for music was something that she couldn't compete with. He was his happiest on stage.

Things at home were far from melodic. Darrell began to stay out all night and pick up extra gigs at the local strip club. Dee feared what he was getting into out there in the streets. When he came home in the wee hours of the night, he barely spoke to her. Darrell felt that Dee shouldn't be singing at a nightclub, he said on several occasions that no respectable wife should be performing there. Dee didn't understand how he could perform at the same club that she performed at, and it was honorable. She didn't care what he thought about it, it was bringing in much needed money to their household.

Gone were the days of the two of them fucking like animals. They were lucky to get it on once a month, in a good month. After being married for over six years, people began to wonder why they haven't had any kids. Shit, Dee even began to question it herself. All that lovin' Darrell and Dee did, something should have come from it. Dee thought that something must have been wrong with them, like they weren't compatible or something. She even felt that maybe God knew their situation and didn't want them to bring an innocent child into it. All their questions were answered on March 6, 1978.

Dee woke up and didn't feel well. She felt like throwing up, and she did. She vomited three times that morning. She thought that it must have been something she ate at the club the night before. For the next few days, her nausea got worse every morning. It felt like she was on a small boat drifting in the sea, being tossed by violent waves.

As Dee hugged the commode, Darrell shouted: "What is wrong with you?"

"I don't know, I feel sick," Dee replied.

"I told you to stop eating those tuna sandwiches at the club, we don't know what meat the cook makes them out of," Darrell said jokingly.

"I don't think it's the food Darrell," Dee said.

"Well, what did you drink last night?" Darrell asked.

Dee replied, "I had my regular, double shot of dark liquor to ease my nerves before I went on."

They both looked at each other, as Dee's head was horizontal to the toilet seat. It was like they both came to the same conclusion, but were keeping each other in the dark. Those couple of seconds of silence said much more than words could have. At that very moment, they knew that they didn't need a test to tell them that they were going to be parents. Love was sowed on infertile grounds.

You cannot force love, either it is, or it isn't. You cannot always choose the path that love takes you on, just hold on tight, buckle up, and enjoy the ride....

Chapter 8:

Trapped With Love

Darlene (Dee) & Mae-April 1978

Sitting on the antique couch that she inherited from her parents, Dee was faced with a dilemma. What to do with this thing that was growing inside of her? She had no desire to let love make its presence known, and she knew that she had to do something fast. She wanted to get rid of love before she felt the pains that it could bring to her. She wanted to evict it, expel it from her. After one month of pregnancy Dee picked up the phone and called the one person that she knew she could confide in, Mae. Mae had always been there for Dee in the past. Unfortunately, Dee's love for herself overshadowed her caring or concern for anyone, including Mae.

Dee picked up her yellow rotary phone and called Mae.

"Hello," Mae answered.

"Hey girl, what you doing," Dee said as if she was really interested in the answer.

"Nothing much, just watching the stories," Mae said in a non-concerned tone.

"What's been going on, what I missed Mae?" Dee asked.

"Dee, what you want?" Mae asked.

"Mae why I always gotta want something," Dee cunningly said.

"Calling me out the blue asking me what I am doing. You know good and well what I do every day at noon, I watch the stories," Mae said.

"Well, you got a minute Mae?" Dee asked.

"It has been a minute already, so you might as well take a couple more," Mae said in a sassy tone.

"Darrell and I have not been happy for months now. We went from having sex every day to rarely. I think that he may be cheating on me." Dee said.

"Dee, the last thing you have to worry about is Darrell cheating on you. That man loves you, he is a real good man."

"I know that, but things have not been the greatest between us," Dee said to make a case for what she was about to ask Mae.

"All relationships have their ups and downs," Mae said in a reassuring tone.

Dee decided to cut to the chase and just tell Mae, "Listen, I have been really sick lately, and I think that I may be expecting."

There was a pause that felt like an eternity. Mae broke the silence and said, "Dee that is good news!"

"I don't want this child. Not right now. This is not a good time or environment to bring a child into. My husband is barely home, and we barely have a pot to piss in and a window to throw it out of!" Dee exclaimed.

"Dee, a child is a blessing from God," Mae said.

Mae's voice began to tremble, the same way it did when she first told Dee that her baby was dead inside of her at the hospital. Dee realized that it was insensitive to even ask Mae what she was going to ask her, but she was her only friend.

"Mae I know you recently had a loss of your own, but you wanted that baby. I have something that is growing inside me that is so foreign that everything inside of me is fighting it off like the flu. I just want to know...... can you go with me to get rid of this baby?"

46

Dee rationalized asking Mae in her mind by thinking to herself, "I would have done the same thing for her if she needed me too." Dee felt that Mae had an obligation to help her in her time of need since she was her friend. All that Dee knew was that she could not do it alone; she asserted to herself that she would not do it alone. Insensitive as it may sound, she didn't care about Mae's reaction. She needed her, and that was what friends did for each other. They showed up in the other one's times of need.

To her surprise Mae said yes, and they went to the clinic the next morning. Looking back, Dee regretted having Mae go with her. Especially knowing that the doctor told Mae that she would never have kids of her own.

Darlene and Mae got all the way to the clinic, and unfortunately they didn't even have enough money for the woman who did them out of her home to perform the procedure. Dee asked Darrell, and he said that he didn't have any money. Dee came to the realization that she was going to have to have the baby. She lit up a cigarette. She inhaled. She exhaled.

Dee has always dreamed of seeing her name in lights but never thought they would become so dim. On October 05, 1978 Davis was born, and a year and eight months later Ren was born June 7, 1980. Dee had a love-hate relationship with the both of them. They were precious boys, so she couldn't help but have some type of love for them, but they were the only things standing between her and leaving the small town to chase her dreams. Darlene felt as stuck as chewed Bubblicious bubblegum stuck to the bottom of some good dress shoes. She was forced to face a love that she never wanted and was not prepared for.

When love comes, you may not be ready for it... but what you do with it is up to you.

Chapter 9:

Asking For Love

Darlene (Dee) & Brennan October 1980

Dee couldn't believe that she was the mother of two snotty nosed little kids. She never could have imagined this life for herself. She always envisioned doing something impactful, like being an actress or a singer on Broadway, not raising kids. She knew some people thought that what could be more impactful than bringing up the next generation? She would tell that same person that living your life kid free has the greatest impact. She believed that children loved you while you were providing for them, and as soon as they were old enough they would leave you lying in your own piss in some nursing home.

She was not an incubator; she felt that she was more than that. Any two people with opposite genital could reproduce. The heroin addict can easily have nine kids, and poor ole Mae couldn't even have one. "Shid, Mae could have my kids, she would be returning them right back to me the first chance she gets," Dee said aloud.

Lately, times have really been hard for Dee and Darrell. She couldn't believe that she was standing on the doorsteps of her husband's brother's house. Dee thought to herself, what kind of man sends his wife to ask his brother to borrow money? What kind of man went gigging every night while his wife and two kids were at home starving, a pathetic one. She didn't like people to know what was going on in her home, so it's hard for her to ask Brennan to borrow some money. It was nothing for Brennan; he had so much of it. He was living the life that she wished she could live. If only that night on the dance floor he would've seen her first, he would've staked his claim on her heart, and she would have never gazed into Darrell's puppy dog eyes. Dee was tired of living the way she had been. She needed something or someone to rescue her. It felt like all the air was being sucked out of her lungs, and she was forced to breathe through her mouth.

Dee felt like she was knocking on Brennan's door for over five minutes. She said aloud as she took another puff of her cigarette, "Where the fuck is Brennan? Shit, he knew I was coming."

"Who is it?" Shouted Brennan.

"Who do the hell you think it is," Darlene replied.

When Brennan opened the door, they locked eyes for what seemed like an eternity. Brennan said," We are around here getting all old, and you are looking better with time."

Dee replied in true Dee fashion, "I just saw you a couple months back, but flattery will get you everywhere with me."

They both laughed. Brennan grabbed Darlene's windbreaker and placed it in his coat closet.

Dee forgot how tall Brennan was. She followed him with her eyes, from the top of his head to his nice plump derrière, his sexy thighs, to his big feet. You know what they say about men with big feet. She attempted to distract herself from the ungodly thoughts she was having towards Brennan. She hummed her favorite gospel song, said the Our Father's Prayer, sung the Alphabet Song, and counted to 100 in English and in Creole. This brother was too fine!

"Would you like something to drink," Brennan asked in his baritone voice.

"Yes," Dee answered, as her voice cracked.

"Oh yeah, you parched," Brennan said jokingly.

They both laughed.

"What would you like, I have water, fruit punch, or orange juice?" Brennan said.

"Orange juice please," Dee answered in a more confident tone.

Brennan walked into the kitchen, as Dee sat on the edge of the sofa in the living room. Everything aroused Dee at that moment. The sound of the ice hitting the glass, the closing of the refrigerator, and even Bree's footsteps on the hardwood floors turned Dee on.

Brennan came into the living room with two glasses, one with orange juice and the other with red fruit punch. He sat both of the drinks on the end table and sat directly across from her. Dee tried to calm herself down because she didn't want him to see her heart beating through her blouse.

Bree handed Dee the OJ, and his hands gently caressed hers as he transferred the glass from his hands to hers.

"So why are you really here Dee?" Brennan asked.

"What you mean?" Dee exclaimed in a sassy tone.

Bree looked intensely into Dee's eyes and asked, "My brother sent you right?"

"No, I came on my lonesome," Dee replied. She thought to herself, "Why did I lie? Why didn't I just tell him the truth. Yes, your good for nothing brother asked me to come ask you to borrow some money so we can make ends meet."

"Ok, then why are you here?" Bree asked.

"Your nephews and I having a hard time getting by," Dee continued by telling Bree about how Darrell spends most of his time in bar rooms, and how he neglects his family. She went on to tell him that she was unhappy. She didn't know why she was so forthcoming with Brennan, she usually kept her business to herself. It just felt right to her to pour her heart out to him. As Dee spoke Bree listened so attentively, it made Dee not want to stop talking. His presence alone was comforting to her. It was like he was her therapist, and wanted her to feel better. As she spoke, he moved closer and closer, like a moth to a burning flame. Dee began to smell Bree's cologne, and it drove her crazy. She just wanted him to just grab her.

Brennan placed his arms around her and told her that everything was going to be okay. Dee melted into his arms just like the ice in her orange juice did on the end table.

Bree whispered, "You always have me, whatever you need Dee, you know Bree got you."

They began to passionately kiss. He grabbed her hand and led her to his bedroom. It was like she was hypnotized and was in a deep trance eagerly anticipating

Bree's next move. They made love, the kind of love that was meant to be. The kind of love that was all wrong, but just felt so right. After they climaxed, they both were so exhausted that they fell asleep in each other's arms.

When Dee woke up, she came to her senses and grabbed her clothes and tried to leave before Bree woke up. As she tiptoed out of his bedroom, he called her name. It scared the living daylights out of Dee. Bree turned on the lamp near his bed and revealed the tears that were cascading down his face. He told her that his only regret in life was not making a move on her, and claiming her for himself. She told him that she shared his same sentiments. Bree got off the bed naked and fully aroused, and led Dee back to the bed and they experienced what could have been. She left with the money that she needed and gained something that she had lost with Darrell, self-love.

There are times when love blurs the lines...
but the fairytale of the boundless pursuit of
love comes with realistic consequences.

Chapter 10:

Preventing Love, Darrell's Secret

Darrell - March 19, 1980

Darrell was the type of man that knew what he wanted but was often distracted in his pursuit of it. His looks often opened many doors that his intellect couldn't. His six foot three athletic frame would make anyone take a double look at him. He was attractive, but not cocky; he was confident. He was a real southern gentleman, the type of man who opened doors or even would throw his jacket over a puddle so that his woman could cross. He was a few years older than Darlene, and because of their age difference tried to assert himself as a father would in their relationship. Dee did not see him that way. He was from a close-knit family, though he never knew his biological father. His best friend was his younger brother Brennan "Bree" who he actually looked up too because of his sense of adventure. Darrell was a hopeless romantic and loved being in love and giving love. Since he never experienced a two-parent household, he yearned to break that cycle by being the man of the house in his own family. Darrell wanted to be the man that his father never was, and the husband that his mother needed while raising him.

Lately, he has not been happy in his marriage with Darlene. She often highlighted his shortcomings and downfalls, and never gave any praise. He was like any other man, yearning to be needed and appreciated. Today Darrell was a man on the brink of making one of the most significant decisions of his life, and sadly he could not consult his wife. He didn't know what was wrong with Dee. It was like she was never satisfied. He sacrificed his career for her and the kids, but it seemed as though that nothing he did would ever be enough for her. He was tired of Dee throwing her family's house that they lived in in his face. When they first got married, Darrell wanted to move Dee to the city, but she couldn't see herself living anywhere but the old run down antique shotgun house that her parents left her. Darrell just wanted Dee to let him love her. She had a way of closing him out when he tried to show her love. The only place where she let him in was the bedroom. Sure, Darrell had his shortcomings dealing with finances, but they always had food on the table.

56

Darrell was disgusted by the way that Dee treated their kids. She treated them like she was babysitting them. She had no real motherly connection with them. After the birth of their last son Ren, Darrell asked Dee to have her tubes tied since she disliked being a mother so much. Dee accused him of trying to take away her motherhood. "Those organs are not what makes someone a good mother, just because you can make a child does not mean you are the right one to raise them." Soon as Dee left the hospital from giving birth, she started back drinking heavily and smoking reefer. She never really stopped drinking while she was pregnant; she just cut down on the amount. Darrell feared that there was nothing that he could do to stop her. Their kids needed a good mother, and she was not one right now. He loved her more than anything, but he couldn't bare to bring another child into this world with her. Living with her was like trying to play a ¾ song in a 4/4 time signature for him. She made him feel like he was one measure or step behind her singing flat in an unbalanced duet.

"I am headed out to help Larry fix his water heater. I will be back in a few hours." Darrell announced as he grabbed his jacket and headed towards the front door.

"You are always on the go these days, you act like I made these kids on my own," Dee said as she lit up a cigarette.

"You know you enjoyed every minute of the process," Darrell said as he grabbed Dee by her waist and held her from the back so that she could feel his manhood on her backside.

"See that's why we have these good for nothing kids now, and God knows that I don't want any more of them," Dee said.

Darrell said under his breath, "me either."

Darrell walked to his car, slammed the car door, turned on the engine and just sat there. Darrell knew that the next few hours would have a lasting impact on their future. There was no going back once he did what he felt he had to do. "It will be just me, Ren, Davis and Dee going forward, I would never have the girl that I always wanted, but this was for the best, Darrel thought to himself.

"Mr. Loving, Darrell Loving." The receptionist yelled through the tiny opening in the glass window.

"I am Darrell Loving," He said in a soft tone to model the appropriate voice tone for the receptionist.

Darrell walked through the narrow white door of the doctor's office and was led to the examination room. The assistant handed Darrell a white gown and asked him who would be driving him home after the procedure. He told her that he was going to drive himself, and she informed him that the doctor would not perform the procedure if he were not confident that he would be able to get home safely.

"Can I use your phone?" Darrel asked the receptionist.

The receptionist exclaimed, "We are on a tight schedule Mr. Loving, all we need is a name. Should I just place your wife's name here?"

"No, don't do that! You can place Mae Jenkins name as the person who will be picking me up, she will be picking me up."

With hesitation, Darrell called Mae so that she would know where he was, and in case something happened to him she could tell Dee.

The assistant left the room, and the nurse and doctor entered. It all went so fast. Darrell walked in locked and loaded and walked out shooting blanks. He took it into his own hands to keep Dee happy. He hoped that Dee would see it like that. He vowed to himself to never tell Dee about the procedure.

> *Sometimes it is good to remove the things that keep you connected to unwanted love. You have to be proactive to protect your heart from hurt.*

Chapter 11:

Confronting Love

Darlene (Dee) Loving - July 1981

Dee treated pregnancy like it was an incurable illness. She never connected with the so-called miracle of motherhood and didn't see what was so special about it. She prayed daily that she would miscarry, and also did things to try to induce it. Dee's, once so bright light felt as dim as a car with one headlight navigating on a foggy night.

One would pose the question of why she kept getting pregnant if she did not want to be a mother? Deep inside getting pregnant for her was a form of self-defeating behavior. She was actually scared of "making it" and leaving the small town and was more like Mae than she realized. She wanted to run away from the horrors that the small town had caused her, but was too scared to. Getting pregnant alleviated her from accepting the fact that there was nothing truly special about her, and she actually wasn't "good enough" to make it. Placing blame on her kids, Darrell, and even Mae was a whole lot easier than accepting responsibility for her shortcomings. Dee's template for the institution of marriage and love was an over-romanticized version of her parent's relationship. Dee ignored all the affairs that her father had, the way her mother neglected her chasing after him, and the circumstances surrounded their deaths. The Carr's household had many deficits and few positives. Dee's experience with love all ended in pain or loss. She accepted that love wasn't love, unless it hurt. She found pain in love, and love in pain.

"Mae, pass me my cigarettes," Dee asked.

"You are almost four months pregnant, and you shouldn't be smoking no way," Mae replied.

Dee said with an attitude, "Don't tell me what I should or should not be doing. I have been pregnant back-to-back since I had Davis in 1979. All I do is run around this tiny house chasing after the Loving boys all day, and not to mention making sure Mr. Loving don't stuff another woman's box."

"Box?" Mae asked.

Dee said in frustration, "Don't act like you don't know what stuffing another woman's box means Mae, sometimes I swear you choose when and where to be all holy moly… well let me put it in terms that you may understand…it's the same thing you put Jimmy out for."

"Why you got to bring up my ex-husband?" Mae said.

Dee exclaimed, "Because I'm not going to sit here and let you act like you didn't know what I meant. Playing stupid is what made him think you didn't know what was going on when he was screwing your neighbor right under y'all roof."

"Well, looks like he is not the only one playing stupid," Mae said.

Dee interjected, "What you mean, what are you trying to say?"

Before Darlene could finish her statement, Mae's voice began to tremble as she said, "You the one who has been pregnant for the past three and a half years, walking around here smoking cigarettes and still drinking, letting the whole world know how these kids done messed up your life, how you could have been somebody if not for the kids. Look at you… you are about to have your third child in a few months, and you didn't even want the first one."

"I am going to stop you right there Mae," Dee said.

"No, you not Darlene! You know how much I prayed to GOD to give me a child, and my prayers always came up void," Mae said.

62

"MAE! I am tired of you bringing that up every time we get into it, GET OVER IT."

"Get over it Dee? " yelled Mae.

"You better stop before your words write you a check that your ass can't cash!" Dee said dismissively.

"I have done nothing but love you... even when it felt like you didn't love me." Mae said as she was on the brink of tears.

"If that what you want to call love, I came into this world by myself and I will die that way. Your love don't pay na'am one of bills in my house. I am all I got."

"You are all you got? Really Dee?"

Dee quickly responded, "I am, no one has ever been there for me when I needed them." Dee knew that this statement was false, but she needed to say something that was going to hurt Mae to the core. In reality, Mae would have moved heaven and earth to make sure Dee was okay.

Mae took two steps towards Dee and folded her arms and said, "No one? I have always been there for you. Don't forget, I was the one with you at the clinic trying to get them to fix your first pregnancy, and your second one, and this one. Luckily, Darrell refused to pay for the procedure. To be honest, he had the money, but who do you think told him not to give it to you and what it was for. In five months you gonna have three babies for a

Negro who could not even hold down a job, and who you don't think know you are expecting AGAIN."

"Now Mae-" Dee tried to stop Mae.

Mae continued, "Now who is the one playing stupid? You play that role better than Hattie McDaniel in "Gone with the Wind," you better believe it."

Dee contemplated slapping the taste out of Mae's mouth, but she had a little girl growing inside of her. Dee thought to herself that if she were not pregnant, she would have made Mae eat her words. She would have knocked some sense into Mae. However, it was hard for Dee to get really angry at the truth. People always said that the truth hurts, but Dee never thought she would feel such a painful blow from her best friend. Every word that Mae said pierced Dee down to the depths of her soul. She had no doubt that she would forgive Mae, but she knew it would be awhile before she spoke with her again. Remnants of that conversation infested their already volatile relationship almost to the point of no resolve.

> *You have to confront love, letting it know what is and what is not acceptable to you. You have to let love know when it has crossed the line. There is a very thin line between love and hate.*

Chapter 12:

The Birth of Love

Darlene & Darrell Loving - December 31, 1981

Ever since Darlene and Darrell's brother Brennan connected sexually over a year ago, things have not been the same between her and Darrell. The two newfound lovers never stopped meeting up, and it has caused Darlene to neglect her wifely duties at home. On top of all that, she was pregnant and feared that the baby girl she was about to give birth to was not Darrell's. She was caught in the middle of two competing feelings, love and disgust. She was perplexed by the idea that this time the baby that was growing inside of her was truly made out of love, but on the other hand not by the sacred consummated love of her husband.

Though she was truly in love with Brennan, her love for him didn't change her mind about being pregnant. She still was disgusted by it and prayed every day that God would remove the baby from her. Even though Dee and Darrell's financial situation did not change, she found solace in the fact that her husband always wanted a baby girl, and this pregnancy would make him happy, at least that is what she thought. She assumed that Darrell would be head over heels when she told him she was pregnant, but Darrell's reaction was a mixture of surprise and anger. He reacted as if she wasn't giving him what he always wanted, a baby girl. Deep down inside she was also worried that he had some suspicion that she was not faithful and that this baby wasn't his.

Love finally wanted to live on the outside of her, so Darrel and Dee took Ren and Davis to Mae's house. Dee and Mae did not say a single word to each other. Dee just looked intensely into Mae's eyes and Mae into hers. It was as close to an apology that Dee could give. Darrel and Dee kissed their children and headed to the hospital.

Dee couldn't believe that she was about to deliver another baby. She thought to herself that finally, Darrell would get to have the girl that he always wanted. It's crazy, but Dee thought that Darrell would have been more excited about this day. Darrell barely spoke to her on the way to the hospital, and had not been emotionally present the whole pregnancy. Dee couldn't believe that she was about to give birth to their first daughter on the anniversary of the day when he first staked his claim on her, December 31. She was about to be the mother of three kids and she knew that she had not been the perfect mother thus far. She gave them all the love that she knew to give.

"Take a deep breath, Mrs. Loving, you should feel just a pinch." The anesthesiologist said in a calming voice.

"I probably won't feel a thing girl, this is my third and final baby. I am getting fixed after this," Dee said.

"You going to do it at the same time of your cesarean section?" The anesthesiologist asked.

"Yea, you won't be seeing me here having no mo' kids," Dee exclaimed as she tried to look at the anesthesiologist while she was lying on her side.

The anesthesiologist said as she helped Dee to sit up in her bed, "Mrs. Loving you are all set. The doctor will be in soon to check on you."

Darlene could feel the epidural starting to work. She felt a cooling sensation that rushed from the injection point up and down her spine. She felt numb from the medicine that the epidural provided, but it was unable to numb the pains of her conscious eating away at her. For the first time in years, she began to cry. It was like all of the sudden there was a switched that turned on, and a movie of all of her faults streamed through her consciousness. She thought about her kids and how she had not been emotionally available to them. She thought about Darrell and how he did not deserve to be cheated on, and not just cheated on, but with his own blood brother. She was in a state of torment, and it felt as if she was having her day of reckoning.

Dee called for Darrell who was standing outside the door of the hospital room. She looked him in the eyes and could not say a word. She just stared intensely into his eyes as tears flowed from her eyes. Darrell kissed her on her forehead and ran his fingers through her hair as he told her that he loved her.

"You still love me?" Darlene asked.

"Of course I still love you," Darrell stated in a reassuring tone.

"I have not been the woman that you deserved these past years, but I promise I will make it up to you. Don't give up on me. Don't give up on us. Don't give up on love."

Darrell interrupted her and proclaimed, "We have both not lived up to each other's expectation of marriage. The greatest gift that we have been given is the opportunity to make things right."

Darlene took a deep breath and said, "I have something to tell you."

Darrell whispered in Darlene's ear as if he knew what Dee was about to disclose, "Whatever you have to tell me can wait, there is nothing more important than what we are doing now, and I don't want you to upset yourself."

Darrell grabbed hold of Darlene's hand and stroked it gently. He began to sing their song.

My girl (my girl, my girl)

Talkin' 'bout my girl (my girl)

I've got…

Dee smiled, and for a moment she felt as if she was back at the VFW hall dancing with Brennan as Darrell sung from the stage.

Dee interrupted her own thoughts as if she had come to some type of profound conclusion and said,

> "I think I know what I want to call the baby. I was going through a baby book and ran across the name Kalila. Kalila means dearly loved. I want this girl to be reminded that she is loved, even when it seems the world has turned it's back on her, shit even when I turn my back on her, she will be reminded. Love is something that I have always had an issue with giving, and I have pushed away many people that tried to give it. So even if I try to push her away, she will know that she was conceived in and born of love."

Darrell looked away to shield his tears and said, "We will always love her, and I will always love you."

The doctor came into the room and asked Darrell if he wanted to stay in the room for the cesarean section. He chose to stay in the room. The doctor began the procedure, and Darrell stood by the side of the bed of the woman that he staked his claim on many years ago. He held her hand tightly and kissed her forehead repeatedly and reassured her that everything would be okay.

As the doctor made his incision, there was a strange series of loud beeps that echoed throughout the room. The doctor stated that everything was fine and that her blood pressure just dropped slightly. A few minutes passed, and the beeps stopped. After what seemed like an hour later the doctor separated the baby and Darlene. Baby Kalila was not breathing. The doctor attempted to revive her, but his attempts were unsuccessful.

Dee pushed herself to an upright position and shouted, "don't die... don't die on me, Kalila... I love you."

Dee felt this uncontrollable urge to fight, to fight for someone other than herself. She stretched her hands out towards her lifeless newborn baby girl and screamed, "don't die!" Darlene screamed from the depths of her soul, and just like that something magical happened. Baby Kalila screamed, and it matched the pitch of her Mother's. As Kalila took her first breaths, Darlene "Dee" Carr Loving took her very last one. Before Dee's death, she felt the intense fervor of love for the very first time.

> *To be successful in Love, you have to understand that love is continuously*

transitioning. Love is everlasting. There is nothing that can break the cycle of love, not even death.

Chapter 13:

Goodbye Love

Mae - January 6, 1982

Just as she did in life, Mae assisted Dee even in death. Mae made the funeral arrangements, notified the family, picked out the casket, made Dee's dress, and even wrote the obituary for her dear friend. Part of her took on this task because she saw how broken Darrell was, and the other part of her did it to compensate for the guilt that she felt about the argument that she and Dee had before her death. Mae never had the opportunity to apologize to Dee for offending her.

Mae looked up to the heavens and said, "Today is the day girl, you ready... this is your last performance."

"Davis help Ren put his shoes on!" Darrell yelled from the back of the house.

"Okay, dad!" Davis replied. Under his breath, he said, "I am tired of helping him."

Davis was five, but he knew better than to talk back to his father. He chased his little brother Ren down and attempted to keep him still enough to put on his shoes.

Darrell emerged from the bedroom dressed in an all black suit with a white button down dress shirt and a crooked black tie. Darrell was dressed to the nines but still looked disheveled. It was apparent that no matter what he put on, his outsides were going to match the way he felt on the inside.

"Let me fix your tie," Mae said, as she stood on her tippy-toes to straighten Darrell's tie, "now that is much better."

"Thank you Dee.......I mean Mae."

How you holding up?" Mae asked as she placed her right hand in the middle of Darrell's back and moved it in a circular motion.

"As tears filled Darrell's eyes he said, "It feels like I am on the inside of a bottle that someone has sucked all the air out of and they won't let me out. I can't breathe Mae, I can't breathe." He held the wall in the hallway as if he didn't, he was going to fall head first to the ground. "I don't know what there is without her."

"I know the feeling," Mae replied.

"She was my light," Darrell said as his deep voice trembled and went up an octave. "She pushed me to want to do better... Mae, I don't know what I'm going to do without her."

Mae interrupted and said, "We got each other, and we will get through this."

Darrell took a deep breath and rested his head on Mae's chest and began to cry hysterically. It was the kind of cry that Mae never seen from a man. She was smitten by his vulnerability and felt the need to console him, just as her friend did. She held the back of his head and pulled him closer to her.

"Come on Darrell, let it out now cause you got to be strong for them kids. They lost their momma, and they going to need you right now."

Darrell cried for a couple of seconds more, then he stood in an upright position to acknowledge Mae's sentiments. Everything inside of Mae wanted to join Darrell and cry hysterically, but she decided to stay strong for him and mourn in her own way. Collectively they both had experienced the lost of someone that they loved so dear, and they would need each other to help heal the wounds of the lost of love. Mae wiped Darrell's tears with her apron and led him to the living room so he could help Davis and Ren to finish getting ready. Mae went to the bedroom to check on Kalila. With all the commotion Kalila was still sound asleep.

74

Mae sat down on the edge of the bed and wrote a letter to Dee to place inside of the casket.

Darlene,

You always find a way to get the last word, you went too far this time! You went and died to win our argument. I can't let you have the last word on this one, NO not this time!

Darlene, where do I begin...you were my first friend... You showed me more love than any man could have. You taught me how to be vulnerable... how to respect and stand up for myself. You had a way of making me laugh, even when I was the one being made fun of.

I just can't believe you are gone...There are so many conversations that we had, and so many that I have hoped to have with you.

Maybe God knew what he was doing when he did not allow me to have any children of my own. He knew that one day I would have to help to raise yours.

Dee.... your daughter, is so beautiful... She has your eyes, and already I can see that she has your spark in them, your desire to be great, and your timeless beauty.

You know that I love you, and I always will.....

Girl, every time that Marvin Gaye's "Heard it through the Grapevine" comes on the radio, I will close my eyes and dance with you.

Your Best Friend,

Mae

Mae told Darrell that God told her to move in to help him with the kids, and to adjust to life without Dee. So, a few weeks later Mae moved into the shotgun house that Dee's parent's left to her. Darrell and Mae both were mourning broken hearts and both needed time to adapt to their new realities. The adjustment was hard for the both of them. Darrell had to adjust to life without Dee whose pessimism gave him the motivation to be better and make her love him. Mae went from being alone, yearning for something or someone to love her, to being in a house with four people who love she would have to earn. It wasn't long before Darrell and Mae started to comfort and console each other inside of the bedroom too.

Mae felt blessed with the opportunity to raise Dee's kids, but they were a constant reminder that she couldn't have any of her own. Mae found solace in the fact that she would be the only mother that Kalila knew, and she was prepared to raise her with the love that she never got to show to her stillborn daughter. Kalila was Mae's chance to prove to the universe that she was capable of doing something that it had robbed her of. Mae was determined to show Davis, Ren, and Kalila the love that their mother Dee was incapable of showing them even when she was alive.

> *Our hearts are wired to remain in a state of balance. A heart that is broken tries to regain homeostasis and heal itself. So be careful not to mistake vulnerability with love.*

Chapter 14:

Borrowing Love

Darrell & Brennan - September 15, 1987

"Ren, Davis, Kalila, come on now! We got to be on the road in the next ten minutes." Darrell shouted while standing in the doorway of their shotgun house.

Darrell watched as Ren, Davis, and Kalila scrambled like ants to get all of their belongings together. They looked forward to spending their summer break at their Uncle Bree's house.

"Don't leave us, we are coming!" Kalila yelled from the dining room.

"Do we really have to stay the whole three weeks there?" Davis asked.

"What are you talking about? I thought you loved going to your uncle's house." Mae interjected from the kitchen.

Davis replied as he looked down at his run-down tennis shoes, "It's not that I don't want to go… I just will miss you guys so much."

Mae propositioned Davis, "If you stay here you are going to have to find a way to help pay some of these bills. Do you want to do that or go and have fun with your Uncle Bree?"

As he placed both hands on his lower waist, Davis said, "I'm not even old enough to work, I'm only eight years old."

Being the oldest of the three children, Davis felt really close to Mae. He could see that Mae was doing her best to be a mother to them. He was old enough to remember the good, the bad, and the ugly with his mother, and her lack of maternal instincts. Davis remembered how Dee sat home all day and cried, and he would never forget the way that she looked at him with disappointment in her eyes.

"I won't have no problem finding something for you to do around here if you were to stay," Mae said.

Davis rethought his plan to stay home and grabbed his clothes and headed towards the door. Mae stopped him.

"I know you are not going to leave this house and not give your favorite stepmom a kiss."

"You are my only stepmom," Davis said as he smiled and leaned over and kissed Mae on the cheek.

Kalila and Ren ran after Davis, and they both kissed Mae on the cheek on their way out of the door. Mae stopped Kalila and adjusted the foil on the end of her beaded braids.

"Be good at your uncle's house," Mae whispered in Kalila's ear.

"I will, I will," Kalila said as she stared at the picture of Jesus that hung in their living room.

"Who loves you Kalila?" Mae asked.

"You, Daddy, my brothers, and Jesus," Kalila exclaimed as she made eye contact with the portrait of white Jesus.

"You got it!" Mae said as she kissed Kalila on the cheek.

They all charged to the yellow and cream-colored four-door station wagon to try to get the front seat. Davis claimed the seat and slammed the door. Kalila and Ren both got into the backseat of the station wagon and eagerly anticipated arriving at their uncle's house.

That twenty-minute drive felt like an eternity to them. They watched as dense tree areas turned into buildings, and buildings turned into skyscrapers. As they pulled up to their Uncle Bree's gated community, Kalila yelled from the back seat, "Can I put in the code daddy?"

"Yes you can, do you remember it?" Darrell replied.

"I sholl do! Its 0-1-4-3," Kalila said in a self-assured tone.

Kalila climbed to the front seat and sat on her father's lap and pressed 0-1-4-3#. When she pressed pound, the telephone rung.

A man's voice answered the phone and said, "Could this be my favorite niece and nephews coming to stay with me for the summer?"

Ren, Davis, and Kalila all screamed in unison, "Yes, it is us!"

There was a beep, and the gate opened for them to gain access to the private community. It was so beautiful. There were trees everywhere. The air even smelled different. For them, it was like the clouds parted and the sun shined directly on his community. It was clear that they were far away from their neighborhood on the south side of town. Before Darrell could even park the station wagon, all of them got out and ran to the front door. Before they made it up the steps, Bree opened the door to greet them.

"Who are you guys? I am looking for my nephews and my niece, have you seen them?" Bree asked jokingly.

"It's us uncle Brennan," yelled Ren.

"You guys can't be my nephews and niece, you guys are too big!" Bree said.

"It's us... it's us," they all said in unison.

Bree asked, "If you guys are really my nephews and niece, what is their favorite food?"

All three of them yelled, "Pizza!"

Bree announced, "Well, that is exactly what I have in the kitchen. Ask Marie to give you guys a couple of slices. I will be in there in a moment, I just have to talk to your father."

All three of them ran to the kitchen to get a slice of pizza from Marie as Brennan and Darrell both walked back towards the station wagon.

"How have you been," Bree asked.

Darrell hesitated, " I've been ok, I guess. Man, I hate to ask you cause you are already doing us a big favor by keeping the kids for three weeks for us but... I just started this new job, and it's promising... but after being unemployed for so long, the paychecks are not coming in fast enough. I just hate to ask, but can you let me hold something until I get paid on Friday?"

"You don't even have to ask. If I got it, you got it," Bree responded.

Brennan reached inside of his pocket and grabbed his wallet, "How much you need man?"

"Whatever you can spare till Friday."

Brennan gave his brother four hundred dollars, "Hope this helps. Don't worry about paying me back. I got a big bonus from the last house I flipped."

"This is too much." Darrell handed his brother back two hundred dollars and said, "I will pay you back on Friday…. Thanks a lot."

Darrell embraced his brother and told him that he loved him, and was thankful for all that he has done for his family. This innocent statement cut Brennan like a dagger through his mourning heart. Brennan knew that he couldn't express how he really felt about Darlene, how he missed her touch, her kiss, and her sex just as much as he did. He had to be a support to his older brother who had a legitimate stake on her heart. It would kill Darrell if he found out that his loving wife and his younger brother were caught up in a love affair for over a year. They both lost the love of their lives on December 31, 1981, when Dee died.

Brennan also had a sneaky suspicion that Kalila was his; Dee told him before she died that she thought so too. What was he to do? Should he publicly claim his daughter and cause even more hurt to his dear brother? Should he just leave well enough alone, and not further tarnish the memories that his brother had for his dearly departed wife? Anyway it went, someone was going to be hurt, and Bree felt that it would be Kalila, so he decided to keep it secret.

Ambiguity in love can protect you from a broken heart, but once clarity comes, the consequences may not be repairable...

Chapter 15:

Love Has No Refund Policy

Ren Loving - September 16, 2002

Ren arrived at school an hour before the financial aid office opened so that he would be one of the first people in line to pick up their refund check when the office opened. Kalila asked Ren to hold her a spot in line, but the line was moving fast for a change, and Kalila was nowhere to be found, and she was not picking up her phone. Ren redialed Kalila's phone number, and it went straight to voicemail. Ren attempted again, and there was no answer.

"Pick up the phone Kalila, pick up the phone," he said aloud as he called Kalila for the fourth time. The phone rang five times and went to voicemail. "I am almost in the front of the line, where are you?" Ren left on Kalila's voicemail.

The auditorium was crowded. It was like a pep rally was going on. There was a sense of excitement and anticipation that filled the room. People were happy, they were smiling, and some were even dancing. There were some dudes from the neighborhood who only dated these girls at refund time, promising to flip their refund check. They were in the auditorium holding the naïve freshman girls' hands and everything. It was funny but to each their own.

"Yo Ren!," Tyrique said as he approached Ren.

"What's up Tyrique?" Ren said enthusiastically.

They gave each other their signature handshake. It went on for like 45 seconds.

"Shit nothing homie, trying to get this paper," Tyrique replied.

"You ain't gone do nothing but trick off to these hoes," Ren said jokingly.

"Niggah that's you all day man. You know I don't love dem hoes. But if Kalila act right I'll spend some of this refund on her," Tyrique said as he motioned as if he was at a strip club throwing ones at the dancers.

"Don't make me beat your ass man," Ren said as he punched Tyrique in the arm and got back in line.

86

Kalila snuck behind Ren and wrapped her hands around him.

"Bout time you made it," Ren said.

"You ain't gonna even give your sister a kiss or say good morning," Kalila said with an attitude.

"I said all that on the million and one voicemails that I left you," Ren said.

"Good morning beautiful, we were just talking about you, and how hard it is to find a good woman," Tyrique interjected.

"Were we?" Ren said.

Tyrique smoothly said, "I was telling your brother that the man that you settle down with will be the luckiest niggah in the world."

Kalila pretended to be uninterested, but she was attracted to Tyrique. He had the prettiest smile, and she could see what he was working with through his grey sweatpants, and she liked what she saw.

Kalila replied, "If you act right you might have a chance. Look, I need my nails done, my hair did, my eyebrows arched, you gone make that happen?" She playfully asked.

"I would take you to the shop, but I ain't paying for none of it," Tyrique said.

Kalila stared and raised her thick eyebrows at Tyrique. She started to tell him where to take the trash he was talking, but he interrupted her when she tried to speak.

"Wait, before you start rolling your neck, let me tell you why. I don't want to interfere with your independence. You are a strong, independent, sexy woman... Did I say sexy? You for dam sure don't need no man to pay for anything for you." He winked and walked away.

Kalila smiled and rolled her eyes.

"For real, where have you been?" Ren asked Kalila again.

"I was helping take down my roommate Amanda braids till like five in the morning and I overslept."

"Kalila you almost had to get at the end of this line." Ren guided Kalila's head so that she could see the line that wrapped around the auditorium.

"No, I wouldn't. That's why I got an older brother. Did I mention you were handsome, just adorable, and my favorite brother."

Ren smiled and said.. flattery will get you everywhere Kay.

The financial aid officer yelled "next," and Ren proceeded to sign out his refund check. Kalila went right after him and signed hers out too. They both went their separate ways and agreed to meet later at the Phi Kappa Mu Pajama Party.

Ren

Until recently no one even knew that Ren Loving existed at Tennessee Mountain University (TMU). But that all changed two weeks ago when the star quarterback was injured in their first home game, and he had to step up for his team. He didn't just step up, he threw 4 touchdowns and led his team to a 35-10 victory against one of their biggest rivals.

Being in the number one spot was nothing new to Ren. All through high school, he was known as Ren the Lover-boy, which was an oxymoron. He just had a way with people. He was much more mature than other guys his age. When he went to parties in high school, he found himself spending more hours talking to the parents of the person who threw the party than his peers. He was sophisticated, classy, and appropriate at all times. He has always done what was expected of him. Ren was 6'4, dark skin, with sleepy brown eyes. His build more suited a basketball player, but he enjoyed playing football.

To quote Kalila, "He gets so much pussy thrown at him." They may throw it at him, but he dodges most of it because of his religious views. He embraced their step mother Mae a little bit more than Kalila did, and shared her love for the Lord. He was a devout Christian who practiced abstinence and was saving himself for his wife. He was in a long-distance relationship with his high school sweetheart Milli who was due to come to Tennessee Mountain University in the spring.

Ren had a true servants heart, he wanted to save the world. He majored in biology at T-Tech and wanted to go to medical school so that he could open a free clinic in his hometown once he graduated. It was out of character for him to go to the Phi Kappa Mu Pajama Party, but his teammates insisted, so he agreed. Though Ren attended the same college as Kalila, they ran in different circles. Ren hung with the "in crowd." It was not like he chased after the popular kids, they sought him. He was likable, and there was something about him that made those who came in contact with him want to know more about him. He was like an open book that was in a language that only he understood. He rarely drank because of a few bad experiences he had in high school while under the influence. Even without alcohol, Ren was always the life of the party.

Chapter 16:

Pajama Jam

Ren Loving - September 16, 2002 09:30 PM

Ren could hear the song, "Lean Wit It, Rock Wit It" as he parked his Jeep Cherokee in the gym's parking lot.

Okay, let's get this over with, Ren said to himself as he turned the key in his ignition to the off position. As much as he wanted to chill with his friends, his thoughts were hundreds of miles away. He really missed Millian, or Milli as he called her. Ren would often find himself sitting and wondering what she was doing back home in their small town while he was out and about in the big city. She was his soul mate.

Before Ren left Louisiana, they were inseparable. Ren was the prom king his senior year, and Millian was right there by his side as queen. He even postponed going to college a year because he wanted to wait for Millian. They were all set to go together, but Milli's financial aid fell through. She has since secured a scholarship, but it will not kick in until the spring semester. He eagerly anticipated Milli's arrival.

Ren decided to call Milli. The phone rung two times, and she answered.

Millian answered the phone, "Hey baby."

"What you doing baby?" Ren asked.

"Nothing, just getting ready to go to choir rehearsal," Milli said.

"Don't tell me they got you doing a solo, GOD said to make a joyful noise," Ren said jokingly.

"And!" Millian interrupted.

"The key word Milli is joyful," Ren said as he laughed.

They both laughed.

"Anyway, what you doing Renny?"

"I'm sitting in my jeep, about to go inside this party?"

"Wait…. you? Going to a party?" Millian said in disbelief.

"What? What you mean, I am always the life of the party? Ren paused, and there were a few uncomfortable seconds of silence.

"What's really going on Ren," Milli asked.

"Milli I miss you, you are one of the only people that really get me."

"I miss you too Renny! I can't wait until the spring so I can come down there and let all those hussies know who man you are."

"Bae, these girls have nothing to give me but a headache, and I already get that from your nagging self."

"Oh no you didn't….. but listen, Renny, I want you to get out of that jeep, go inside that party, and let all dem hussies see what they can't have. I want them so jealous when I get down there." She laughed, and then finished with, "keep your hands off of them though."

"I'll try," Ren replied in a sly manner and then disconnected the phone call.

Ren opened the jeep's door, stared down at the long johns underwear he was wearing, took off his shirt to show his washboard stomach, and walked towards the Gymnasium. When he entered the dimly lit gym, he looked around to see if he saw Kalila, and show nuff he

93

did. She was face down ass up in the middle of the dance floor. He thought to himself, "Why did she always have to be so extra?" When she lifted her head, she motioned for her brother to join her in the middle of the dance floor, and he did. Kalila and Ren were just over a year apart, so they did everything together. Ren would die if anyone found out that he and Kalila had a dance routine to the song "Up Jumps Da Boogie," by Timbaland & Magoo. Kalila and Ren did what they have always done every time music played, they partied. Music was in their bloodstream. Their bodies instantly reacted to a drumbeat or a bass chord. Before they knew it an hour had passed, and they never left the dance floor.

"Ren lets take a shot," Kalila shouted over the music.

"Nah I'm good Kay."

"Come on, just one. Take a shot for me. Let's turn this place out bro like back home," Kalila said.

Ren thought back on the conversation that he had with Milli in his jeep, and he also wanted to show his team members that he wasn't lame. Ren hesitantly said, "Where dey at?"

Before Ren could change his mind, Kalila headed to the makeshift bar and ordered two shots of Everclear. One shot led to two, two led to three, three led to four. Ren felt like he was floating, and everyone that was around him was moving much faster than he was. Ren saw Tyrique & Malcolm from the team and attempted to give

94

them both their signature handshake, but he messed it up horribly.

"I am out of here Y'all," Ren said as he began to walk to the door.

"Kay, you going to let that niggah drive like that?" Tyrique asked.

"Ren hold on," Kalila shouted to get Ren's attention.

"Malcolm, can you bring my brother home?"

"What I look like that black dude from driving Ms. Daisy?" Malcolm asked.

Tyrique looked Malcolm in his eyes, motioned at Kalila's butt with his eyes, and asked again, "Go on and make sure he gets home safe, I'll come get you after the party."

Malcolm took Ren's keys and led him to the parking lot. Malcolm helped Ren get into the passenger side of his jeep.

"Man, I am not drunk, I can drive," Ren slurred.

"I know man, just let me take you home," Malcolm said.

Malcolm and Ren drove off as Kalila and Tyrique danced until they turned on the lights in the gymnasium.

Chapter 17:

Random Love

Kalila Loving - September 17, 2002, 02:35 AM

Kalila led Tyrique into her pitch black dorm room. Without sight, they navigated the room motivated by the anticipation to bone.

"You got to be quiet, you are going to wake up my roommate," Kalila whispered softly as her soft lips rubbed gently across Tyrique's ear. She felt all the tiny hair follicles on his ear that were all at attention, responding to the sounds of her alto voice. That wasn't the only thing that was at attention. Kalila felt his erected manhood through his jeans as he thrust it against her. It was like all the blood left Tyrique's brain and ended up in his pants, and all that was on his mind was putting it inside of her, and she was okay with that. Casual sex was all Kalila wanted, and she hoped that he would keep his mouth closed and not tell Ren about their encounter.

Kalila whispered, "Tyrique you are making too much noise."

"I will be telling you the same thing after we get started," Tyrique asserted.

Kalila and Tyrique were all over each other, they were like untamed animals in heat. Their tongues intertwined as they ripped each other's clothes off. They almost tripped over the basket of clothes that she neglected to fold earlier, but it did not throw off their mating dance.

Kalila looked around the apartment, and her roommate Amanda wasn't there. She turned on her five-disk CD player and hit next until it stopped on her legendary freak-um mix. Kalila threw Tyrique on the bed, and climbed on top of him and moved to the tempo of the song "Stroke You Up," by Changing Faces. Kalila loved being in control. Having sex for her was just that, sex. Kalila removed the emotionality from the act and embraced the pleasure that it brought her. When it came to men, she was always the aggressor, but it turned her on that Tyrique chased her. Kalila was uninhibited when it came to sex, she was like a primal man. She saw what she wanted and went for it. Will Kalila hook up with Tyrique after tonight? If he put it down right, maybe.

Kalila was only twenty years old and had no quorums about making her own decisions. She definitely didn't follow the crowd, she ran from them. She didn't believe in labels, especially prescribed gender roles. She believed that a men and women were the same in all aspects, they just had different sexual instruments. She was her own woman living her life the way she wanted to, she was free.

Being sexually uninhibited did come with some repercussions for Kalila. She didn't have too many female friends other than her roommate Amanda. Most girls saw Kalila as a whore or someone that was after their man. Her voluptuous body didn't help things either. She was 5'10, 140 lbs., with a caramel complexion that looked like it was kissed by the sun. Kalila oozed sexiness. Anything that she wore made it look like she was intentionally trying to be sexy, and that was not the case. Kalila's hair was short, dark, and curly. She used to have long hair, but after a break up her senior year of high school she went natural by cutting all the perm out of her hair. When Kalila walked into the room, even if you didn't like her you would find yourself staring at her. She often tried to downplay her beauty by wearing oversized clothes and not wearing any makeup. Little did she know, trying to conceal her beauty made her even more attractive. Being as beautiful as she was you would think she was overly confident, but that wasn't the case. She was bound by her many insecurities.

After Kalila and Tyrique finished, he went to the bathroom and wiped up, then he left. Kalila went to sleep satisfied in the pool of sweat and love juices.

Kalila woke up thinking that she had overslept, but it was only six o'clock in the morning, and she still had three hours before she had to be on campus to recite a poem for her communications class. This was nothing new for her, she waited until the last minute for everything, and she has become quite skilled at doing things the last minute.

Kalila got up from her bed, changed her sheets, and then took a shower to wash away last night's escapades and try to clear her mind. After her shower, she put on some jogging pants and an oversized shirt and jumped right back into her full-size bed. She stared up at the ceiling fan for what seemed like an hour, watching it go round and round. She couldn't muster up the energy or the motivation to start writing the speech. She was having trouble finding a single word to write down. She decided to turn on the radio in hopes that she would be inspired or even distracted.

Kalila reached under her bed and grabbed an old sneaker box. She placed the box on the top of her bed and opened it. She searched passed her vibrator, condoms, headphones, old batteries to find her stash of weed. Kalila removed the seeds and rolled the joint as tight as a hooker's dress on the first of the month. Before long the room was filled with smoky clouds of weed smoke. She placed a towel along the bottom of her dorm room door to trap the smoke and lit incense to help to mask the pungent smell.

Kalila said aloud, "Oh that is my song," as she turned up the volume. She began to sing the song...Say my name, by Destiny's Child. Kalila thought about last night and how she had that niggah Tyrique calling out her name, and how she could still feel him inside of her.

It was just what she needed; school had really been stressing her out. Tyrique's stroke game was good, but after all that talk, he only lasted ten minutes once she got on top of him. He lasted longer than most though. Kalila has been told that if she bottled her stuff up and sold it, she would make a killing. When she got on top, it was a wrap. She loved controlling the pace, the intensity, and the depth. For Kalila there was nothing like watching a man turn from Barry White to screaming like Tevin Campbell, talking about slow down I'm about to cum. Last night Kalila freely gave Tyrique her good loving, and he freely gave her his.

Kalila placed her pen on the paper and wrote the first thing that came to her mind...

-Death....

She thought to herself, "No, I can't write about that... my classmates already think I'm weird and this will confirm it." Kalila's antagonistic thoughts were succumbed by the motion of the pen that flowed across the paper from left to right. She was familiar with and has had many experiences with death. Death welcomed her into this world, and she was infatuated by its supremacy.

Kalila flirted with death intentionally and unintentionally a few times of her own. She was born dead, not breathing for almost one full minute. She stopped breathing while swimming in her Uncle Brennan's pool when she was nine and had to be revived. She attempted suicide three more times before the age of eighteen, two times by overdose, and two years ago by cutting her wrist. When she saw the blood shoot from her arms, she fainted and hit her head on the sink of the bathroom. It left her with a small scar above her eyebrow. She almost died that time. Kalila loved life, but loved flirting with death.

Kalila's family tried everything to deter her from attempting suicide. Mae told her that she would go to hell if she did it. Mae couldn't understand why someone with so much life ahead of them would even consider killing themselves. Kalila felt that Mae was constantly forcing the Bible down her throat and that only pushed her further and further away from the blue eye GOD that Mae called Jesus. Kalila wasn't an atheist by any means, she loved and believed in a higher power. It was that same higher power that she called on when she was at her lowest, and she knew that it was because of it that she was still alive. She knew and believed that there was a GOD, but not all the extras that came with being a Christian. It killed Mae that Kalila did not see GOD as she saw him. She was genuinely concerned for Kalila's soul. Darrell told her that she was too pretty to be trying to hurt herself, and her brothers Davis and Ren just pretended that the attempts never happened.

Kalila has been through it all. She had been hospitalized, prayed for, baptized, lectured, and even evaluated; but nothing removed her urge to die. Tomorrow was the two-year anniversary of her last attempt, and she did not feel like "wanting to end it all," which was big for her. Like they say in narcotics anonymous, she lived "just for today."

Before she knew it, the poem was completed. She titled it, "Life's Converse," since the converse or opposite of life is death.

> *Life's Converse*
> *I'm infatuated with you*
> *Oh I think I love them*
> *I want to wear them all the time*
> *I bet I would have one of my best games in them, no overtime*
> *Life's Converse*
> *You are my lucky shoes; I just have to close my eyes and take that shot*
> *Life's Converse*
> *These are the only shoes that ever really fit me like a glove, it's like they are a part of me...*
> *Life's Converse*
> *It's been two years since I wore you, you have been missing*
> *I looked everywhere, and I couldn't find you, even under my bed*
> *I can't wait till you come back to me like Cinderella's glass slipper*

*I am ready, waiting, anticipating the day
destiny slides you on me......*
Life's Converse
*I guess it's true what they say that opposites
attract*
*Like magnets placed together facing
opposing poles*
I am drawn to you
Life's converse...

Chapter 18:

The Awakening of Love

Ren Loving - September 17, 2002, 07:30 AM

Ren was awakened by the sunlight beaming through his blinds, wearing only drawers and a wife beater. Ren looked around his room and tried his hardest to remember how he got home. He remembered bits and pieces of last night's party. He recalled how he and Kalila killed the dance floor and how he took way too many shots of Everclear. He remembered all that, but couldn't remember the most crucial detail of how the hell he got home? Who dropped him off? Who took his clothes off and tucked him into bed? While lost in his thoughts, he heard someone snoring on the floor beside the bed. He looked around the room for some sort of sharp object just in case he had to fight off whoever was in his room. He peeked over the bed, and there was

Malcolm, laying on the floor shirtless, wearing only his basketball shorts balled up in a fetal position. He looked cold as hell.

All of the sudden Malcolm rolled over on his back, and he was fully erect. Ren did not wake him, he leaned over the bed to get a better view. Ren let his eyes scan Malcolm's entire body. As the ceiling fan blew, he smelled hints of Malcolm's cologne.

Malcolm was six foot tall and two-hundred and fifty pounds. Most would describe Malcolm as a thick dude. If he didn't play football and had a couple more meals, he would be closer to fat. Malcolm's cold black hair had waves that would make the most experienced fisherman sick. He was a man's man. Malcolm was the star fullback of their football team who had one of the fastest one hundred and ten yards in the conference. Ren leaned over the bed and attempted to make out the numerous tattoos on Malcolm's chest and arms. Ren watched as Malcolm's chest inflated and deflated which caused him to become erect as well.

Malcolm suddenly opened his eyes, exposing his hazel colored pupils. Ren quickly rolled over and pretended to be still asleep.

"Yo homie," Malcolm whispered in a deep voice.

Ren rolled over and said, "What's up man, How did I get home last night? The last thing I remember was dancing at the party."

"I took you home man, you were pretty wasted," Malcolm said.

"I could handle my liquor man, I wasn't wasted," Ren said defensively.

"Then how the hell you got home Ren?"

"Well thanks, and you tucked, I mean put me to bed too?" Ren asked.

They both laughed.

"Niggah, ain't nobody tucked your ugly ass into bed, I threw your lanky self in that bed and was too tired to go home," Malcolm said.

"Never know these days, people are taking advantage of people," Ren said.

"Niggah, I ain't no fag." Replied Malcolm.

"Good! I ain't either, I got a girl!" Ren said as if he was trying to convince himself.

Malcolm said as he stood up, "Me too man, so scoot over, my back hurts from sleeping on that hard ass floor."

Ren scooted over to the right side of the bed and turned on the TV.

Ren said in a serious tone, "Really thanks again bruh for taking me home, and making sure I didn't do nothing crazy."

"Crazy, like what?" Malcolm asked.

Ren replied, "just nothing crazy, like being tucked in bed by some strange ass niggah. You probably read me a bedtime story and put baby powder on my chest."

They both laughed. Malcolm punched Ren on his shoulder, and they began to play fight in Ren's full-size bed. Malcolm ended up on top of Ren and pinned both of his hands down to the bed.

"Talk all that stuff now," Malcolm stated.

Suddenly, Malcolm and Ren's laughter abruptly changed to silence as they stared intensely into each other's eyes. Ren could not control his physiological response to the horseplay. Malcolm felt it and made his move.

While Malcolm was on top of Ren holding down his hands, he whispered in Ren's ear, "I wanted you in your right mind, and I wanted you to remember me, that's why I didn't make a move on you last night. Truth be told you were all over me last night bruh."

Ren began to try to fight Malcolm off of him, but when Malcolm released his hands, he stopped fighting. Ren closed his eyes and kissed Malcolm. Ren didn't think about Millian as his lips met Malcolm's. Everything Ren knew to be true would tell him that what he was doing was wrong, but it just felt right to him in the moment. What he had been saving for Millian, he freely gave away to Malcolm. He was no longer pure, he was no longer innocent, he was no longer a virgin.

After they climaxed, they both went into the bathroom and shared a hot towel.

Malcolm looked Ren square in the eyes and said, "Don't tell nobody about this," as he wiped the head of his penis and put his basketball shorts back on.

"Niggah, who am I going to tell?" Ren said as he looked away.

As Malcolm moved closer to Ren he whispered, "Cool! See you at practice later. Don't worry man everything will stay the same. Don't trip off of what we did."

"Man I ain't tripping," Ren said, but he knew that everything would be different for him, he wasn't the same.

"This won't be the last time we fuck around right?" Malcolm asked.

Ren wanted to tell Malcolm that it would never happen again, but his curiosity wouldn't allow him to. He wanted to hold Malcolm's hand and pray that God removed the intense emotions that they felt for one another and that he (God) would forgive them for their ungodly transgressions. But instead, he answered, "Nah man, it won't."

Chapter 19:

The Love Interrupted

Davis Loving - September 17, 2002

Davis woke up in a cold sweat. His heart was beating a mile a minute.

"What's wrong, you had one of those dreams again?" Millian asked.

"I am going to be okay, I'm just going to get a glass of water."

Davis's dreams were getting more and more vivid. He went to his medicine cabinet in search of his anxiety medication. Davis popped one into his mouth and chugged it down with a handful of faucet water from the sink. Davis splashed cold water on his face and looked at his self in the mirror. He took a couple of deep breaths as he held on to the edge of the sink. He repeated to himself, "it's not real, it's not real." His anxiety began to ease, so he went back to bed.

"I'm sorry about that, I didn't mean to wake you."

"Is there anything I can do baby?" asked Millian.

"No baby, you being here really helps to calm me down and get me back to my center," Davis replied.

Millian laid her head on Davis's chest and began to rub her fingers through his chest hair. She listened to his heartbeat and felt its pace decreasing.

Davis and Millian both knew what they were doing was wrong, but they felt as if they needed each other. They both filled a void in each other's lives. Their love affair began when Ren went off to school. Millian needed someone to talk to, and Davis provided a listening ear. Through many late night conversations, they found that they had a lot of things in common. They both loved their small town and loved to sing. There was no question that if Ren found out about their love affair, he probably couldn't go on, so they both agreed to keep it from him. The problem was that they were getting more and more serious, and it was becoming harder and harder for them to keep their love secret.

"Are you going to family day next month at TMU?" Davis asked.

"I have to go. Ren would flip out if I didn't make it. That is all he has been talking about."

"I am going too. It's going to be hard for me to keep my composure if he kisses you in front of me Milli."

"Well, at least you know that's all we will be doing. He is still a virgin and wants to stay that way until he gets married, well when we get married."

"Don't play with me," Davis said.

"My last name will be Loving, but not cause of him."

Davis pulled her close to him, and they began to passionately kiss.

"I got something that would put you to sleep, and it is even better than that nerve pill you just popped."

"What is that?" Davis asked.

Milli lifted the comforter and tucked her head underneath. She kissed Davis's chest and licked him until she reached his outie bellybutton. She grabbed his semi-erect penis and began to perform oral sex. Davis stopped her and warned her that he didn't shower before bed. She peaked her head from underneath the blanket and whispered, "That's the way I like it."

Davis Loving

Davis loved his family, but from a distance. Though he lived only a few minutes from his dad and stepmom, he rarely visited them. He felt that he needed some time to himself, so in his own way, he pushed them away. Oddly enough, the strongest connection that Davis had with his family was his brother's girlfriend, Milli. She kept him abreast of what was going on with Kay and Ren, all the while shielding him from their judgments. He began to withdraw from them after he graduated from high school. He was proud of his brother and sister, but felt like he received the short end of the stick. He was forced to go to work right after high school, and college was not an option for him because of their financial situation. He had no interest in college no way. Davis was a mediocre student but would've liked someone to ask him what he wanted instead of forcing it on him.

Davis was everything that Ren wasn't. He was rebellious, bold, and rough around the edges. He had a few run-ins with the law, but thanks to his Uncle Brennan, none of the charges stuck. Just as he did for Kalila, Uncle Brennan was a lifesaver for him. Davis blamed the world for most of his misfortunes, that was until a few months back when he started having panic attacks and was referred to a therapist.

Once he started going to therapy he began to take accountability for things and wanted to take steps to repair his broken relationship with his family. While in therapy a lot of stuff from his past was dredged up. The things that he had tried to push out of his consciousness were resurfacing. He kept having the reoccurring dream of watching Kalila drowning in his uncle's pool when they were younger, and how his Uncle Brennan did not let him go out and save her. In his dream his Uncle made him watch her drown. Every other night he had the same dream.

His therapist recommended hypnosis, so a few weeks back he went in for a session. While hypnotized he was guided by the hypnotist to that day at the pool. It was like he was watching a movie, and he was the star. Davis saw his 11-year-old self sitting on the couch inside of Uncle Brennan's house playing Nintendo with his uncle. Davis could hear Ren and Kalila outside playing in the pool. Davis smelled the scent of chlorine that was carried in through the open window. The smell of chlorine was then overpowered by the scent of his Uncle's cologne. His happiness and excitement were interrupted by a state of confusion. The next thing he remembered was his brother yelling for help and his uncle Brennan running out to perform CPR on Kalila. He remembered feeling helpless and frozen with fear watching from the glass patio door. On that day his Uncle Brennan revived his sister, but at the same time suffocated a piece of him.

Chapter 20:

Reclaiming Love

Kalila Loving - September 10, 2003

It is true what they say that love changes you. It was not until Kalila met Tristan that she realized that love did not have to hurt. Tristan made her want to be a better person. He accepted her, flaws and all. He wasn't concerned about all the dudes that she had sex with before him. Tristan was confident that he had what it took to keep her, and that she wouldn't go looking for no one else. Tristan's confidence was what initially drew Kalila to him, but his sensitivity is what has kept her with him.

For the first time in a long time, love finally felt good to Kalila, not just sex. She felt loved in and out of the bedroom. Tristan came into her life at a time where she was spiraling out of control. In search of this thing called love, Kalila looked in many places. She looked in the club, the bottle, threesomes, deep inside of other girl's pussies, and even in death. Kalila finally realized that she was neglecting the most important person in the love puzzle, herself. She gave sex too much power over her life and often mistook it for love.

Tristan has shown her the healing power of love, the power of giving and receiving love. Two years ago if you had asked Kalila if she was going to stop having sex cold turkey, she would have cursed you out. She still viewed sex as something beautiful, but she has gained a new respect for the act. She decided to save her stuff, her "good pussy" for her future husband.

When she met Tristan last year, she actually tried to give him some on the first night that they met, but he rejected it. Instead, he held her and asked her a million and one questions about herself that she didn't think that anyone really cared about but her. She told him everything, every single detail. She didn't want him to find nothing out about her past from anybody but her. The last thing she wanted was one of his friends talking about they smashed, and cause him to feel some type of way. This man knew everything about her, from her crazy ass family to her love affair with death. Tristan never judged her, and through all her shit he still loved her.

Kalila's journey of self-love was inspired by the love that she saw in Tristan's eyes for her, but it has been perpetuated by the love that she has grown to have for herself. Abstinence hasn't been easy for her; she was always horny. The right gust of wind against her nipples or up her skirt would cause her to almost reach a full orgasm. After getting her hair done last night, she had a dream that she was having sex with her gay hairstylist, and his boyfriend caught them.

Since Kalila stopped having sex, she has had to relieve her stress in other ways. She started working out and has lost a couple pounds and inches in her waist. She also started attending church. Yeah, she has been going to the house that "White Jesus" built. Kalila's stepmom, Mae would be so proud. She even joined the school's gospel choir. Kalila felt that "White Jesus," was not all bad, but there something about him that she just didn't trust. He looked sneaky to her.

Lately, Kalila has been trying to keep herself super busy. The busier she was, the less time she had to think about sex. She even spent the days that she didn't have class volunteering and bringing pleasure to those in need, to keep her from going home and pleasuring herself. Abstaining from sex was a full-time job without a W-2.

What have you done for me lately………

Lately, Tristan has been pressuring Kalila to have sex with him. He turned every conversation that they had toward sex. Everything that he said or did had a sexual undertone. Tristan has become the polar opposite of the guy who just wanted to hold her at night. She knew that it had been a long time, but she hoped that he understood

116

that there was nothing more that she wanted to do than to please him, but she had to get herself together without the complications of sex. She had just differentiated sex and love, and she didn't want to get them confused again. Tristan has been making abstaining from sex hard for her. Often when they laid together, he would thrust his hard dick up against her, and in those times Kalila had to pray to "White Jesus" for strength.

Kalila was glad that Amanda decided to join her in the fight to reclaim their pussies. Amanda was a God sent. Every time Kalila thought that she was going to break, she reminded her of how far she had come. Kalila was low key proud of herself. Her whole life has been about controlling things that she had no control of. This was something that was under her control, and no bad could come from it. Kalila needed Tristan to jump back on board with it though because if he placed his big dick on her again, she didn't think that even "White Jesus" could keep her from it.

Kalila loved the new her. Her search for love has ended, because not only has she found it in Tristan, but she has also found it inside of her.

> *You have to love yourself first before you are truly capable of loving someone else.*

Chapter 21:

Messing Around With Love

Ren and Malcolm - September 15, 2003

As Malcolm and Ren were leaving football practice, they stopped at Ms. Jenkin's Burgers. This was their daily stop after practice, especially since she took their campus food debit card. Ms. Jenkin's burgers were so big that most people couldn't finish them. The only thing that was bad about visiting Ms. Jenkin's Burgers was that when you left you smelled like old grease. Malcolm and Ren have become close friends over the past year, and they have been able to successfully keep their not so drunken secret, secret. They have tried numerous times to stop "messing around" with each other, but they always found themselves back in each other's arms.

"Numba 115 and 116," Ms. Jenkins yelled in her deep, shaky voice from behind the counter.

Malcolm and Ren went to the counter, picked up their food, and found a booth at the back of the small smoky restaurant.

"What are you doing later dawg?" Malcolm asked.

"Just watching TV, I don't have no major plans. Why what's up?" Ren asked as he looked at Malcolm with squinted eyes, "What you trying to get into man?"

Ren knew what Malcolm's question meant. He wanted to connect again. Just the inquiry into his day aroused Ren. Truthfully it has been all that Ren had been thinking about, he yearned for Malcolm's touch.

"You already know what I want to get into," Malcolm said as he slapped the back of Ren's head.

"Man you play too much," Ren said angrily like he really didn't enjoy the horseplay.

"I thought we agreed that last time was the last time man," Ren said as he dodged Malcolm's slaps.

"Come on man, you know we say that shit every time we mess around. I just agreed to that shit cause it makes you feel better," Malcolm said.

Ren paused and turned really serious. His guilt has really started to get the best of him. He didn't know how much longer he could live these two dueling lives. The more he and Malcolm connected, the less he looked forward to connecting with his girlfriend, Milli. He prayed that he could go back in time and resist Malcolm's initial advances, but he knew that wasn't what he really wanted. He interrupted his own thoughts, and asked, "Where is this going to lead. We both know that we ain't gone be no couple or nothing, so what are we doing?"

Malcolm did what he always did when Ren was trying to address a serious issue, he turned it into a joke. "You trying to lock me down, you trying to put a rang on it?"

"Get out my face," Ren exclaimed as he looked Malcolm in the eyes and smiled.

The truth was that the both of them were not ready to deal with what the future held. Ren believed that if he continued this ungodly relationship, he would fall out of God's grace and couldn't enter the gates of heaven, at least that is what they taught at his church back home. Malcolm has developed strong feelings for Ren, but he knew that deep down inside that what they had would never be more than sex. They both had significant others, and they both had tough, hard, decisions to make to ensure that they did right by love.

Love is often found where you least expect it.

Chapter 22:

Three is a Crowd

Kalila, Tristan & Rieko - Sept. 15, 2003

"Hey baby," Kalila said as she walked through the door of Tristan's small studio apartment.

"Hey, Kay-Kay," Tristan said as he stood up from the sofa and met Kalila halfway between the couch and the front door. They gave each other three small kisses on the lips as they embraced each other.

"How was your day?" Tristan asked as he grabbed Kalila butt cheeks and pulled her closer to him.

"Better now that I am here with you," Kalila replied.

"Y'all mother fuckers need to get a fucking room," yelled Rieko as he exited the bathroom.

"This is my spot niggah. If you don't like it, you can let the doorknob hit you where the good lord split you," Tristan said.

"Well, its definitely time for me to go if y'all niggahs gonna to be doing that all in my face," Reiko said.

Tristan grabbed Kalila tighter and dipped her like they were doing the tango, and kissed her again.

"You lucky I don't feel like catching the transit home," Rieko said as he threw a pillow off the sofa at the loving couple, but missed.

Rieko was Tristan's best friend. They did everything together. They had been friends since grade school. They both played for TMU's basketball team, just as they played side by side all their lives. The two of them were different as night and day. Tristan was clean-cut, preppy, and cultured. Rieko was uncultured, vulgar, and had no couth.

Reiko had long dreads and tattoos that covered the majority of his body, which was one of the things that Kalila actually found attractive about him. Tristan and Kalila went with Reiko to get his last tattoo to celebrate his twenty-second birthday. Reiko got a black angel surrounded by snakes. He has been getting a tattoo every year since he turned 16 years old, it made one ask the question, "who the hell and where the hell was his mamma?"

As different as they were, they were inseparable. When I say they did everything together, they did everything together. They played basketball together, took most of the same classes, and damn near lived together. Their relationship was a testament that the age-old saying birds of a feather flock together was not true. Reiko and Tristan might have flocked together, but they were different in all the ways that really mattered.

"She got a key now?" Rieko asked.

"Niggah, why you worried about it? Are you jealous you don't have one?" Tristan said sarcastically.

"Man, I don't want no key to this place! Who needs a key to this studio apartment when I got the key to your heart." Rieko said and jokingly as he closed his eyes, puckered up, and pretended to kiss Tristan.

Tristan dodged Rieko's playful kiss, "Man get the hell away from me with all that."

They all laughed.

Kalila got so used to having Rieko around that when he wasn't it felt strange. She even considered Reiko when her and Tristan did romantic things together. When she made dinner at Tristan's crib, she made enough for Rieko. He was actually a good distraction for her. Whenever things got hot and heavy with Tristan, she used Rieko to unknowingly cock-block Tristan's sexual intentions.

Truth be told she liked Rieko. After their many conversations, which he called "shooting the shit," she found that he was a big softy. Kalila and Tristan would talk for hours about nothing. Kalila saw why Tristan was so fond of him, and why they were ride or dies. One night at the beginning of her and Tristan's relationship, Reiko made a pass on her. He tried to kiss her while they were both drunk alone in the kitchen. It never happened again, so she never told Tristan.

Tristan didn't need any more hurt in his life. Tristan's mom abused drugs, and she did anything for her next hit. She supported her habit by selling the only thing that she owned, her body. Tristan's mother even used drugs while she was pregnant with him. While Tristan was attending high school, there was a rumor that the football team ran a train on her. Tristan shielded his ego by doing the only thing that he knew to do, immersing himself into basketball. Playing basketball was his escape.

Tristan didn't know his father, he was rumored to be one of his mother's many Johns. Tristan was raised mostly by his grandmother. His grandmother taught him the importance of showing women respect. She was all the family that Tristan had. Unfortunately, she died three days after he was accepted into Tennessee Mountain University. Rieko was all the family that he knew, and they were more than friends. They were brothers.

Chapter 23

New Love Sowed

Davis & Milli - September 26, 2003

Milli sat on the edge Davis's porch anticipating his arrival. So many thoughts fluttered her mind, as she tried to make sense of it all. Milli thought to herself, that she was too young for this, and what will happen with her relationship with Ren once he found out. Milli was already disappointed in herself because she never made it to TMU, she had to stay home to take care of her bedridden father.

From a distance, Milli saw Davis's blue Dodge Neon pull into the driveway. Milli's heart rate doubled its normal pace. She was so nervous. She couldn't even look at Davis as he opened his car door and approached her.

"What was so important that you needed me to leave work? Did something happen to your dad or the family?" Davis asked.

"No Davis, everybody is ok," Milli replied.

"Well then what is it? You sounded really cryptic over the phone," Davis said as he approached Milli.

Milli looked away and said, "I'm late Davis."

"Where are you late to Milli, where are you trying to go?" Davis asked.

"No, I am late….. late…… Davis." Millicent said as she looked down at her stomach.

"You pregnant?" Davis asked.

"I took two test, and both of them were positive." Milli proclaimed.

Davis walked passed Milli and went inside. Milli followed him.

"You got to be shitting me," Davis said as he paced back and forth.

"What did you think would happen," Milli shouted.

"Not this Milli, that was the last thing I thought about while we were having sex. I thought you were on the pill," Davis asserted.

126

"I told you three months ago that I stopped taking the pill, it was making me sick. I wanted us to start using protection, but you insisted that we do it raw!" Milli shouted.

"What are we going to do about this situation?" Davis asked.

"What do you mean? I ain't getting no abortion!" Milli said with conviction.

"I am not saying that Milli, but we have to do something. Look, I got an idea. Let's call my brother up and tell him that you are pregnant by way of some type of immaculate conception," Davis said sarcastically.

"Davis stop!" Milli yelled as she held her head.

Davis interrupted, "You haven't even had sex with Ren so how in the hell you gonna explain to him that you are pregnant. Fuck it, it's time to tell him anyway, we been hiding this shit for too long Milli!"

"I ain't ready for all that Davis," Milli said as she began to cry.

"You ain't ready for what Milli? What is your end game? Cuz Ren is a big boy and its time that we keep it real with him about us."

Love in the dark comes to the light.

Chapter 24:

Love Heist

Kalila Loving - October 17, 2003

"I can't believe that it is almost Thanksgiving, and next semester we'll be graduating," Kalila said to Amanda as they exited choir rehearsal.

"Yeah, three and half years have come and gone," Amanda said as she buttoned her oversized windbreaker.

Kalila grabbed her jacket and hymnal and followed Amanda to the door. "Girl I am not looking forward to going home for Thanksgiving. My stepmom thinks she can cook, but in reality, she barely boils water correctly."

"At least you have somewhere to go for Thanksgiving Kay, both of my parents decided to go on a cruise… without me. Aint that some stuff? My dad just got his settlement from his accident he had 3 years ago, so nobody can't tell them they ain't rich."

"Now you know, you are welcome to come home with me. Ren is driving, so you know he gonna be blasting gospel music all the way there," Kalila said.

They both laughed as they exited the recital hall.

"You headed home?" Kalila asked.

"I have to use the bathroom, so I'm going to go to the engineering building on the seventh floor. That's my duck off spot when I have to really use the bathroom really bad."

"Well good luck with of all of that," Kalila said jokingly.

The two friends embraced as they went their separate ways. It was a beautiful night out, so Kalila decided to walk back to her dorm room instead of taking the shuttle. It was only five blocks from the recital hall. As she walked through the dimly lit campus, she began to sing the song they were rehearsing, "Silver and Gold," by Kirk Franklin.

She didn't know it, but she sounded just like her mother when she sang. If you closed your eyes, you would have thought that it was Dee singing, not her. It's crazy how genes and DNA works. How you can pass something as small as a singing voice along to someone that you have never had the opportunity of meeting. Kalila found strength in singing. She loved the way it made her feel and the impact that it had on others. Singing was in her blood, and it was singing that has gotten the Loving family through many situations. Her father Darrell taught her to sing through her tears, fears, joys, and disappointments.

As she walked back to her dorm, she took a deep breath of air and reveled in her new discipline self. Every step she took, she felt more empowered, and for the first time in a long time she felt complete. A car pulled up behind her with their high beams on. She turned around and put her hand above her eyebrows to shield the light from her eye to catch a glimpse of the car that was behind her. The car's light became brighter and brighter as it came closer and closer to her. She felt a little uneasy about how slow the car was driving down the narrow street. Kalila thought that the vehicle was campus police, and she wondered why did they have on their high beams. The car finally passed by her, and her anxiety decreased.

Out of nowhere, Kalila heard someone call her name. She looked around, and there was no one there.

"I know I am not crazy," she said aloud as she picked up the pace in her walk.

Everything around her seemed to be moving. The trees swaying side-by-side looked as if someone was chasing her. The rumbles of leaves against the ground and shadows from the streetlights haunted her every step. She had a gut feeling that something was wrong. She felt her heart rate increase, and she had to take deeper breaths to compensate.

"Kay!" Someone shouted again, but she was able to make out the direction in which the person was. She looked towards the sound.

As she turned to acknowledge that someone was calling her name, she was hit on the back of her head with a wooden object. Kalila fell to the ground. She tried to get up, but someone pushed her back down.

"Help me!" Kalila screamed.

"There is nobody here to hear you scream," a man dressed in all black said as he covered her mouth.

"You know what I want... You going to make me take it?" He asked.

"Please, please, please don't hurt me," Kalila pleaded with the masked man as she tried to fight him off of her.

"You can make this hard, or you can make it easy," he said as he ripped her skirt off and pulled her panties down past her ankles.

Kalila bit his hand, and he slapped her unconscious. He dragged her lifeless body beside the adjacent building near her dorm and began to rape her. She came to but was paralyzed with fear. She remembers him staring into her eyes as he had his way with her. He finished, and then he whistled, and two other guys came from behind the tree, and they all took turns raping her lifeless body.

She just wanted them to remove themselves from her sacred place, and not take away her love. They left her unclothed, beaten, bruised, and battered. She felt so dirty and an overwhelming sense of embarrassment. Every part of her body ached, but the part of her that hurt the most was her heart. She was ultimately found an hour later by campus security, and she was taken to the hospital. She left the hospital before she could be examined.

For the first time in years, that intense feeling to escape overtook Kalila. She wanted to find comfort in death, but instead, she began to pray.

Chapter 25:

Blaming Love

Kalila & Amanda - November 10, 2003

Kalila felt like she was encapsulated in a deep dark hole and she couldn't pry herself out, no matter how hard she tried. It has been almost a month since the rape, and she could still feel them inside of her. She could still taste their sweat as it dropped slowly on her lips as they thrust themselves inside of her lifeless body. She could still hear their laughs as they passed her around like a blunt on a Saturday night. The sounds of their grunts and moans still echoed through her ears, keeping her wide awake most nights. After what seemed like one million showers, Kalila still somehow felt so dirty. She felt useless and abandoned. She asked herself, what did she do so wrong in her life that "White Jesus" would let this sort of thing happen to her? Every time she took one step in the right direction it was like something always tried to pull her back; she didn't think there was no way she could back from this. She was just getting her life together, and now she felt as though there was no reason to go on. She didn't consider committing suicide because she felt as if she was already dead on the inside. She told Tristan and Amanda about the attack, and they were the only reason she had not "offed herself."

Tristan reassured Kalila that the rape was not her fault, but she still blamed herself. You never know how much someone loves you until something comes along and test the very foundation of it. She had never had someone who loved her like Tristan did. Tristan refused to let her be alone in her dark bedroom, he spent every night there, holding her in silence and waited until she was ready to talk about the attack. Tristan has been her lifeline, and if she doubted his love for her, after this it was clear.

Tristan persuaded Kalila to report the incident to the police, but by then all the evidence was gone. He even found her an assault victims support group and went to the first meeting with her. As she told her story to the women and their partners, he held her and even cried before the end of it. She hadn't even given him any of her love, and he empathetically listened and empowered her as she recounted how three other men violently took her love away. Kalila only remembered bits and pieces of the rape, and she actually hoped that the parts that she did remember God would cause her to forget. Going through this she knew that Tristan was the man that she

134

was meant to be with, and the differentiation between love, pain, and sex was never so apparent.

Hurt can't be easily replaced with love. Until you are truly healed from the hurt, it will always resurface.

Chapter 26:

Love Comes Back home

The Loving's - Thanksgiving 27, 2003

The Loving family came together every year at Thanksgiving time. No matter where each one of them were in the world, they always made it home to Baton Rouge Louisiana for Thanksgiving. Coming home to that small shotgun house for them was something that they looked forward to. This year was different though, they had more than just food that they were bringing to the table. They all had their own shit going on in their personal lives that weighed heavily on their hearts.

They all should have received Academy Awards for their performances around that oblong wooden antique dining table. If awkward silence could be measured, it would weigh a ton. The skeletons in each one of their closets would scare the hell out of even a Halloween enthusiast. There was a culture of silence that shaped their relationships, so many things out in the open but yet went unseen. Love was present but absent when it really counted.

There was so much deceit in that tiny dining room of that shotgun house. Davis had to pretend that he and Millicent were only friends, and Ren had to pretend that he was still in love with her. Mae had to pretend that she was not thinking of her baby Nidra, and Darrell had to pretend he wasn't missing Dee every waking moment of every day. The biggest pretender of them all was Kalila. She had to sit at the table and pretend that she hadn't experienced one of the most traumatic things that have ever happened to her and that she was not carrying remnants of that traumatic day inside of her.

"Let's say grace," Darrell shouted as everyone sat around the table. "Who is going to say grace this year?"

"I'll say grace dad," Ren said as he grabbed and squeezed Milli's hand tight.

"Everyone, please bow your heads," Ren stated as he looked around the dining room to confirm that everyone's eyes were closed.

Heavenly Father,

We come to you today to give thanks. We want to thank you for all you have done for

137

us. Thank you Lord Jesus for another opportunity to be in a room full of the people in the world that I love the most. Please bless the food and the hands that prepared it. Please let this food be nourishment to our bodies. AMEN.

"That was a long prayer. I am starving bro, I have been working at the shop all day," Davis shouted from the other end of the table.

Ren laughed and said, "You have to take time to thank God for all he has done for you man."

"Bro, God knows my heart," Davis said.

"Your heart Davis? You still have to take time to thank God for what he has done. I know for certain that prayer really changes things and makes things happen. I prayed that God send me a god-fearing woman, and he sent me Milli. I thank the lord for her every night. I am going to pray that God sends someone like her into your life and maybe you would not be so irritable."

The whole table laughed. Davis laughed the hardest because he knew who Milli really belonged to. Milli smiled awkwardly and kissed Ren on the cheek as she said, "I love you."

There was an awkward silence that consumed the room. Ren got out of his seat and reached inside of his pants pocket. He grabbed Milli's hand and assisted her out of her chair. He looked deeply into her eyes and said;

"Love is a journey that everyone is not fortunate enough to take. Love is having the understanding that the focus of love may not be perfect, but it is in the imperfections that make you love them more. Milli, I have loved you from the first day I laid eyes on you, and I can't see a life without you by my side. I'll be your Adam, and you'll be my Eve, I'll be your Boaz if you'll be my Ruth."

Ren got down on one knee. He opened the black box and said, "Milli, just like the women I named in the Bible, will you complete me by being my wife?

Milli began to cry. She stood there looking down at Ren as he gazed into her tear filled eyes. She looked around the room and made eye contact with Davis. They stared at each other for what felt like a minute. Her heart was pounding so fast, she did not know what to do or what to say. She was in love with the brother of the man that was on one knee vowing to love her for eternity.

Davis was enraged. If you were standing next to him you could feel the heat coming from his body. He wondered what was taking Milli so long to say NO. If looks could kill, Milli was already dead.

You could hear a pin drop in the room as everyone eagerly anticipated Milli's response.

"What's your answer baby?" Mae enthusiastically shouted from the other end of the table.

"Yes…. Yes…. Yes, I will marry you!" Milli stated as she broke eye contact with Davis and shifted it towards Ren.

Darrell and Mae both hugged each other, as Mae shouted, "Welcome to the family baby."

Kalila got up out of her seat and hugged Milli and Ren as they embraced each other. It was apparent that Davis was not happy with the proposal, and most of all Milli's acceptance. He tried to smile, but all he was able to muster up was a look of disgust. He approached the happy couple, and looked them both in the eyes and said, "congratulations." He informed them that he had to get back to work, and they would celebrate later when he got off.

Milli had to choose between her love for Davis and not wanting to hurt Ren. At that moment she had to choose between what type of life she wanted to live. She knew that Davis meant well, but he was barely making ends meet with his job at the shop. She knew that if she married Ren, she would have a life that her parents couldn't give her, and she couldn't do for herself. She was perplexed, but yet settled into her decision. The downside was that she knew that she could not stop seeing Davis because of her love for him. She also knew that love did not pay the bills. It also made the decision of whether or not she was going to keep Davis's baby easier. She knew that there was no way that she could move forward with Ren while being pregnant.

"Did you know he was going to do this?" Milli asked Kalila.

"Girl, I had no idea he was going to propose. I would have given you a heads up because from the looks of those nails you had no idea," Kalila said jokingly.

"You better leave my nails alone," Milli said.

"No for real girl, how does it feel?" Kalila asked.

Milli whispered to Kalila as she looked down at her modest engagement ring, "My heart is pounding so fast. I feel as though it's going to jump out of my chest. I have always dreamed of getting married, but I didn't think it would happen so soon. Ren didn't even give me a hint that he was thinking about proposing to me."

"I know both of you guys can't wait until that wedding night. You guys probably going to need an instruction manual on how to even have sex." Kalila said jokingly.

They both laughed.

Kalila leaned closer to Milli and said, "No seriously, I think it's cool y'all going to wait until marriage. These Niggahs ain't no good out here. Lord knows I wish I could take my virginity back and give it to Tristan."

"How are you guys?" Millie asked.

"I know that man loves me, that's all I can say," Kalila said with certainty.

In all of the excitement, Kalila forgot about all of her troubles. While talking about Tristan, and their love she was reminded of all the things that she forgot. She was back in that old shotgun house, but this time she didn't come back alone. Both Milli and Kalila had more in common than they knew. They were both contemplating the decision of whether or not to keep the love that were sown inside of them. One was sowed in love and the other in hate.

Kalila had to talk to someone about the rape, and she needed someone to help her get rid of her unwanted baby. She decided to have a conversation with her stepmom. Only if Kalila knew that if her mom had her way she wouldn't have been here, and it was Mae who saved her life. Just as Mae did for Kalila's mother Dee, she agreed to take her to the abortion clinic in the morning to get rid of the baby.

Being around people that love you can temporarily make you forget about the lack thereof.

Chapter 27:

Getting Rid of Love

Mae & Kalila Lovings – November 28, 2003

The next morning Kalila and Mae went downtown to the abortion clinic. They sat in silence as Kalila filled out the paperwork for the procedure. Mae looked around the small doctor's office and thought back to the time that she sat in an office just like it with Kalila's mother, Dee. She disagreed with abortions, but in her stepdaughter's case she believed that it was the best option. Mae held her tiny travel Bible in her hand, closed her eyes and began to pray as if she would open them and not be in their current situation. Though Kalila showed no emotion, Mae knew that she was hurting on the inside. For Mae, having a child was such a blessing, even under these unfortunate circumstances.

"Are you almost finished with the paperwork?" Mae asked.

"I just got one more signature," Kalila replied.

"How you feeling baby?" Mae asked.

"I just know that this is something that I have to do. I know I couldn't live with myself or even look at the baby," Kalila said.

Mae said in a last ditch effort to prevent Kalila from going through with the procedure, "I know it's hard for you, but have you thought about the possibility for adoption?"

"I know you don't agree with this, but I have made up my mind," Kalila said firmly.

"I am here to support you baby in any decision that you make," Mae replied.

Kalila began to cry. As tears rolled down her eyes, Mae whispered in her ear, "God will forgive you for this."

Mae grabbed hold of Kalila's hand and pulled her towards her. She wrapped her arms around Kalila and placed her head on her chest. She ran her fingers through Kalila's short curly hair and hummed "Amazing Grace." Mae was interrupted by the nurse who called Kalila to the back. Kalila was given some pain medication, placed her feet in the stirrups, and the last thing she heard was suction. Just like that, she wasn't pregnant anymore. Mae

144

helped Kalila get dressed, and waited in the recovery room with her.

"I'm ready to go," Kalila said with tears in her eyes.

"Then let's go baby!" Mae said.

Mae and Kalila gathered up their things and headed back to the waiting room. Mae went to the nurse's office to sign Kalila out while she waited in the waiting room. While in the waiting room Kalila made eye contact with someone she knew all so well. At first, she thought that Milli was there with a friend that sat beside her, but when she heard the nurse call Milli's name, she knew that she was there for the same procedure that she just had.

Kalila thought to herself, how was she even pregnant, if she was saving herself for Ren? If she wasn't having sex with Ren, then who was she having sex with? Whose baby was she at the clinic aborting? Mae entered the waiting area right after Milli left. Mae did not see Milli, and Kalila decided not to tell her until she got more information as to why she was there. Milli definitely had some explaining to do.

Chapter 28:

Unearthing Love

Kalila & Davis, December 1, 2003

Kalila Decided to stay in Baton Rouge an extra couple of days. She needed more time to wrap her head around what had happened to her. Even though it was not Tristan's baby that she aborted, she felt an overwhelming sense of guilt for going through with the procedure. She knew that it was the best thing that she could have done, but it was still hard for her to deal with. Kalila found comfort in laying in her old twin bed at home. Home was the place that she felt most safe. She found refuge from the pain in the shotgun house that her grandparents left to her mother. She looked around the room and somehow the place that seemed so huge to her when she was younger, now felt so small. As she reflected, she heard a knock on her bedroom door. It was Davis.

"Come on in D," Kalila said as she sat up in her bed.

"Kay it is 2 PM, why are you in this dark room with all the blinds closed?" Davis asked.

"I'm okay, I just been tired lately," Kalila replied.

"Well it's time to get your tired ass out of bed, I need your help with something," Davis said as he pulled the comforter off of Kalila.

"What Nah! What you need that can't wait till I get up? I'm trying to get my beauty rest," Kalila said jokingly.

Davis paused and got really serious, "Well, I have been seeing a shrink."

"Bout got-damn time! Your ass has been crazy," Kalila said as she wiped the sleep from her eyes.

Davis asserted, "Come on Kay, I'm serious. He gave me an assignment. I have to tell someone about what happened to me, something from my past" Davis said as he sat on the edge of the bed.

"Well, What is this assignment that you need my help with?" Kalila asked.

"I've been dealing with some issues from my past that are still messing with me Kay," Davis said as he looked away from Kalila.

Kalila moved from the head of the bed and joined her brother on the side of the bed. She placed her hand on his shoulder and sat there in silence until he was ready to speak.

Davis continued, "I have been having a hard time sleeping cause I've been having these weird dreams."

"What kind of weird dreams?" Kalila asked.

"Remember the day at the pool, the day you almost drowned Kay?"

"Yeah I remember," Kalila replied.

"Well, I keep having dreams of you drowning. I have to watch you drown every time I go to sleep Kay," Davis said as tears flowed from his eyes.

"I am still here, I didn't drown," Kalila reassuringly said to Davis.

"That's why I went to see somebody. Reliving that day at the pool has been torture for me. I even went to a hypnotist about it." Davis said and waited for Kalila's reaction. He knew that she would have something smart to say.

"A hypnotist?" Kalila asked.

"Yes Kay, a hypnotist. I actually was able to go back to that day at the pool, and I found out the reason why I keep having those dreams."

"What was the reason?"

"While you and Ren were out in the backyard swimming. Uncle Brennan and I were playing video games," Davis said.

"Ok," Kalila said to speed Davis along in his storytelling.

"Uncle Bree touched me Kay," Davis said.

Kalila was lost for words. With disbelief, she said, "He did what?"

"He did Kay, that was the first time, and it wasn't the last time." Davis placed his head in his hands to disguise his tears. "You are the only person that knows this Kay. I had to tell someone. It was killing me on the inside."

As she attentively listened to Davis's story, she began to remember things about her own attack. She saw flashes of white light, and just like that she was back to the day of the attack. She was laying on that cold, dirty ground perpendicular to her apartment building. She was fighting one of the perpetrators, and she remembered tearing one of their shirts and seeing a tattoo. She vividly saw a symbol of an angel and snakes. She began to cry.

Davis began to console her, and said, "I knew you would believe me, Kay.... I knew you would believe me."

"I feel so free Kay, it just felt like I was stuck in a bad dream. He was like a father to us, and I just never thought…..." Davis cried as he held Kalila.

"Did he touch you too Kay? Did he?" Davis asked in anger.

"No, he never touched me. I am so sorry that that happened to you Davis. I am so sorry that you had to carry that burden with you all these years."

Kalila knew all so well what it felt like to carry a secret deep down in the pits of herself. She felt relief in the fact that Davis found his freedom from the secret that bound him, but she didn't know what to tell him other than she was sorry. She wanted to let Davis know about the rape but didn't have the strength to.

The news that her Uncle Bree molested Davis rocked her world. He was one of the only constants in her life. She wanted to believe Davis, but she couldn't see her uncle that she revered so much committing such a heinous act. She refused to accept it or even let the thought of her Uncle Brennan hurting Davis slip into her consciousness, though deep down inside she felt what her brother disclosed to her was the truth.

Chapter 29:

Graduating Love

Kalila & Family- May 13, 2004

The Dean of the College of Communication approached the microphone and announced, "Would the candidates for the Bachelors of Arts degree in the College of Communications please stand. Please hold all your applause until all the graduates of the College of Communications names are called."

Kalila stood up proudly and adjusted her black gown. She looked into the audience and tried to make eye contact with each one of her family members. Everyone came out to support her, Darrell, Mae, Ren, Milli, Davis and Uncle Bree.

She stood behind the stage and reflected on how much she had been through, and how much she had changed over the last four years. She has grown from a little country bumpkin to a sophisticated woman. She felt a sense of accomplishment as she eagerly awaited her name to be called by the Dean. She was also happy that she was graduating with the love of her life, Tristan.

She was in a good place. She followed Davis's lead and sought counseling. She even found the courage to tell Tristan about her flashback about Rieko. He reassured her that Rieko was with him on the day of the incident, and when she brought it up in her counseling sessions, her counselor told her it was common to relive the event and add people that were close to her into her memories.

Kalila was at peace with the decision that she made to abort the baby, and felt that her life was now finally on the right track. She even promised Tristan that as a graduation present, he was going to get some, which made him very happy. It had been well over two years since she had sex with anyone consensually.

Kalila said to herself, "White Jesus, I am happy. Please don't let nothing fuck it up."

Kalila waited patiently as the Dean called the last names A through K. She took one final look into the crowd and teared up. She thought to herself, "I am really about to graduate."

The dean called, "Kalila Amara Loving."

Most families adhered to Dean Michaels instruction to hold their applause, but he didn't know her family. He didn't know that they anticipated this graduation day since the day she enrolled at Tennessee Mountain University, and showing out at graduations, parties, baby showers, and even bat mitzvahs was a Loving family tradition. They all wore matching t-shirts with Kalila's face on it. Mae brought the entire congregation of her church and anyone who ever knew Kalila or her mom from Baton Rouge. As soon as the dean called Kalila's name, she heard a thunderous roar from the crowd, and she knew it was her family. Mae was hitting a pan that she snuck in, and it sounded like she was speaking in tongues. The rest of her family started a chant, and the only thing that Kalila could make out was..... Ka-ka-lil-lah, I know you feel her.

Kalila felt embarrassed and proud at the same time. Deep down inside she wanted them to show out for her, she worked hard for that degree. After the graduation, they decided to go to Le'Perin's Seafood to celebrate. Kalila was looking forward to being the center of everyone's attention, but was nervous about how everyone would get along at the table. This was going to be the first time that she saw her uncle since Davis's confession, and she hadn't seen Milli since they both were at the abortion clinic.

Le'Perin's Restaurant

"I am here everyone," Kalila yelled as she placed her hands on her hips and pranced inside the private room of the restaurant that her Uncle Brennan reserved.

Everyone stood up and applauded. As Kalila passed each person around the table, she was greeted with heartfelt congratulations and tight embraces. The only person that was missing from the dinner that was special to Kalila was Tristan. His family also came to town and they were having dinner at another restaurant. They made plans for later that night. Kalila was surprised that Malcolm showed up to her dinner because he and Tristan were close as well. She attempted to greet Malcolm with the secret basketball handshake, but it was an epic fail.

When Kalila got close to Mae, Mae reached out her arms to her and pulled her close to her. As Mae hugged Kalila, she whispered in her ear, "You are the spitting image of your mom, and I know that she would be so proud of you right now."

This made Kalila tear up. She whispered to Mae, "You did an alright job raising me. I hope that you are proud, cause you are the only mother I know."

Ren interrupted, "Enough of all that, it's time to celebrate," as he raised his glass of tea in the air and initiated a toast.

"I know you ain't gonna make no toast with no tea, let's get some champagne," Brennan said as he motioned for the waiter to come over to fill their glasses.

Darrell stood up and said, "I would like to make the toast for my baby girl."

The waiter filled their glasses, and they all faced Kalila as Darrell began his toast.

Darrell gathered his thoughts and said,

> *"There is no love like the love a father has for his daughter. When you were born, you changed me. You made me evaluate every aspect of my life. I wanted to make sure that I was the example that you measured every man in your life by. Your birth was a present, an unexpected gift that I did not deserve. I received something that I didn't know I was capable of accepting." He looked Kalila in her brown eyes and said something that confused her, "I was the only father you knew too."*

Kalila laughed it off as if he was mocking her and Mae's conversation.

Brennan interrupted, "Everyone let's celebrate Kalila."

Everyone raised and clanked their glasses together.

Kalila gazed across the table and made eye contact with Davis. She could feel his anxiety, sitting in the same room as the person who caused him so much pain. From across the room, she mouthed "thank you" to her brother. She knew that the only reason why he came was to celebrate her. He mustered up a smirk and winked at her.

Since the proposal, Milli and Ren were joined at the hip. They virtually finished each other's sentences, and it appeared that they were deep in love. On the outside, they looked like the perfect couple, but Kalila knew that Milli was harboring a deep dark secret. Milli's guilt was apparent by her lack of eye contact with Kalila the whole night.

All of a sudden, Darrell and his brother Brennan exited the room. Kalila could see them passionately discussing something through the glass door of the private room. Minutes later they both walked back into the room, and they were different. The only thing she could make out was her father Darrell saying, "you had to get her that." Kalila believed that it was because whatever her Uncle Brennan gift was, it must have been better than her father's. She was used to her Uncle Brennan showing him up, and she thought that he would be used to it as well.

As Darrell and Brennan entered the room, Kalila shouted, "Now where are my gifts?"

"It is that time right," Brennan said as he looked at Darrell.

156

"Yeah, it is," Darrell replied in a melancholy tone.

"Your father and I put our heads together, and decided to combine our efforts to get you something really nice," Brennan said.

"I like the sound of that," Kalila said with anticipation.

"Where is it?" Kalila said as she looked around the room.

"Well, we have to go outside to see it," Brennan said.

Kalila raced to the front door of the restaurant. Everyone followed her. She was met at the front of the restaurant by the maitre'd who handed her a small envelope with a set of keys in it.

"Close your eyes baby girl," Darrell said as he placed his hands over Kalila's eyes and said, "don't peek."

He walked her to the side of the restaurant and removed his hands from her eyes and said, "now look."

Kalila opened her eyes and saw a 2002 gold 4 door Maxima with leather seats. She was overjoyed, to say the least.

"Dad lets go for a ride," Kalila looked at Darrell and exclaimed.

Darrell looked at Brennan and said, "Take your Uncle Bree for the first spin."

Love shows up, even when its hard.

Chapter 30:

The Night of Love

Kalila & Tristan – May 13, 2004 8:00 PM

Kalila was on top of the world. For the first time in a long time, she saw a light at the end of the tunnel. She was on a high from all the love that her family showed to her at her graduation party earlier that day. She eagerly anticipated spending some time with Tristan later on. She meticulously shaved her legs, trying to walk away with little or no cuts. She was unsuccessful. She jumped into the tub to wash the day off of her. While lying in the bathtub, she fantasized about what was to come when Tristan arrived. She yearned to feel him on the inside of her and wanted nothing more than to prove to him that she was well worth the wait. She yearned to fulfill every one of his sexual needs and desires.

Lost in her thoughts, she submerged her hand in the bubbly water. She began to place her fingers inside of herself, but was disturbed by a knock on the door. At first, she thought that the knock was coming from the bathroom door, but after screaming "who is it," she realized that it was someone at the front door. She dried off with a towel and wrapped herself in her bathrobe. She looked through the peephole, and it was Tristan's best friend, Reiko.

"Give me a minute, let me put some clothes on," Kalila shouted through the door.

"Aight," Rieko said as he waited patiently outside the door.

Kalila ran to her bedroom and grabbed the first things that she saw to throw on, some basketball shorts and an oversized t-shirt. She ran back to the front door, and let Reiko in.

"What's going on Reiko?" Kalila asked.

"I got to talk to you about something, I gotta get something off my chest," Reiko said as he stood at the front door with both hands in his pockets.

"Could you have just called?" Kalila asked.

"No, this is a conversation that I had to have with you in person Kay."

Reiko walked into the apartment and sat on the sofa. He gazed around the room as if he was looking for something or someone. "Are you here by yourself?" He asked.

"No, Amanda is in her room," Kalila said. She was really home alone, but there was something about this whole visit that didn't sit well with her.

"If I tell you what I have to tell you, I need for you to promise not to get mad. I'm serious. You got to promise that you will not be mad at me, and you will forgive me," Reiko said in a serious tone.

"What do you mean, get mad at you? What could you have possibly done that will make me that mad at you?" Kalila asked.

"You gotta promise me," Reiko whispered as he gazed into Kalila's eyes.

"I promise, I won't get mad. Just tell me what you have to say!" Kalila said so that Rieko could get to the point.

"I am not a bad person. I know I'm a little rough around the edges, and a little hood, but that does not make me a bad person. Kay, I just can't continue to face you every day knowing.... You didn't deserve that. Nobody deserves that," Reiko said with conviction.

"Deserve what? What are you talking about? You are starting to scare me now!" Kalila said.

Reiko continued, "It was all his idea. He didn't think it was fair that you were making him wait to have sex, and before him you gave it up so freely. It was supposed to be a joke, but when he hit you over the head with that piece of wood."

Kalila interrupted Reiko, "What are you saying?"

"We were just supposed to scare you. He took it too far," Reiko said.

Kalila asked, "he who," as tears filled her eyes.

They both were interrupted by a knock on the front door. Reiko placed his hand on his lips, grabbed his hat and hid in the living room closet. Kalila gathered her composure and walked slowly to the door.

"Who is it?" She said as her voice trembled.

"It's me…. baby." She looked through the peephole, and it was Tristan.

In that moment she did not know who to trust. She had a sneaking suspicion that Reiko was there that night, but Tristan denied it. She thought to herself that this must be some sort of sick joke. What was in it for Reiko to come clean? Why now, after all these months?

She sent Ren a text message urging him to come over right away, and she was in danger, just in case they tried something. She opened the door, and let Tristan inside of the apartment. She wanted to get to the bottom of it. She wanted to prove to herself that she was not crazy. She wanted to find out what really happened that night, and who was responsible for taking her love.

Tristan entered the room. He grabbed Kalila by the butt cheeks and gave her the customary three kisses on her lips. Kalila's anxiety was at an all-time high. Her knees were so weak, she could barely remain standing. Her heart was beating a thousand miles per minute. It felt like she was having one of those bad dreams that you can only awaken from by calling the name of Jesus.

"What's wrong baby? You seem tense," Tristan said as he rubbed Kalila's shoulders.

"I'm okay, just have a lot on my mind," Kalila said has she separated herself from Tristan.

While inside the closet Reiko accidentally knocked over a pair of shoes. It made a thunderous noise.

"Did you hear that?" Tristan asked as he walked towards the closet.

"I didn't hear anything. Let's sit on the couch so we can talk," Kalila said in a persuasive manner.

Tristan ignored Kalila's request and walked over to the closet to investigate. He opened up the closet and saw Reiko trying to hide behind Kalila's winter jacket. He grabbed Reiko, pulled him out of the closet, and threw him to the floor.

"What the fuck are you doing here man?" Tristan yelled.

Reiko attempted to respond, but Tristan continued. "I should have known you guys were messing around. Don't think that I never noticed the way you mother fuckers look at each other."

"Tristan it ain't even like that, he just came over to talk to me," Kalila said.

"Talk to you? Then why the hell is he in the closet. People I know that go to their "friend" houses don't typically hide in the closet when their dude come over. People that are hiding something do that kind of shit," Tristan said as he walked away from the closet and closer to Kalila.

"It's not even like that man, I just came over here to talk to her. I hid in the closet because I knew you would think something," Reiko said.

Tristan yelled, "Nah, you didn't get enough right? You had to come back to try to get some more."

Suddenly it all made sense to Kalila, but never in her wildest dreams she would have imagined that the love of her life was one of the individuals that took her love so violently from her. An overwhelming sense of fear overtook her and she did not know what to expect next. She already knew that they were capable of violently raping her, and wondered what was to stop them from doing it again, are even worse, killing her. She prayed to herself that someone would save her. She felt trapped, not just in her small two-bedroom dorm's apartment, but in love.

"What are you going to do, kill me?" Kalila said as she approached the kitchen.

"No, I came over here to tell you what happened and that is it, Kay. I'm not going to let nothing happened to you." Reiko said in a sincere tone.

"If the both of y'all said what y'all had to say, please leave," Kalila said as she quickly grabbed the sharpest object she could find, a butcher's knife and pointed it at Tristan.

Tristan said as he slowly approached Kalila in the kitchen, "Now you know I just can't leave Kay. What would stop you from calling the police? More importantly, you promised me some tonight, and I don't want you to break your promise. You always said you were a woman of your word."

Tristan lunged toward Kalila and grabbed the butcher's knife. He threw the knife across the room and pinned both of her hands behind her back. He lifted Kalila up and carried her to the sofa. He pinned both of her arms down and got on top of her. Kalila tried to fight Tristan off of her, but he was too strong. Kalila could feel him becoming aroused by her resistance.

"Get off of me you freak!" Kalila yelled as she called out to Reiko for help.

Tristan whispered, "What makes you think that my brother would choose a bitch over me? If he knows like I know he better get ready to get some of this good pussy too. That pussy good too."

Reiko stood behind Tristan and watched as he pulled down Kalila's basketball shorts and attempted to insert himself inside her. Reiko struck Tristan over the head with the lamp. Unfortunately, the lamp just bounced off of his head and did not slow Tristan down.

Tristan turned and looked at his best friend and said, "Niggah, I'm going to excuse you for that one, now come grab her hand."

Rieko usually did what Tristan asked of him, and this time was no different. Reiko held Kalila down, as he looked away. They were interrupted by a knock at the door.

"Campus police open up." Someone shouted.

Kalila screamed, "Help me…. I am in here…. Help me."

The police officers kicked down the door and gained entry into Kalila's apartment. Tristan and Reiko were both taken away in handcuffs. A few minutes later Ren arrived. They held each other tight without saying one word.

Chapter 31:

Confronting Love II

Davis & Brennan – May 15, 2004

I am going to do this. "I can't let this have any more power over my life," Davis said to himself as he pulled up to the gate of his Uncle Brennan's house. Davis felt that it was time that he confronted his Uncle Brennan for the years of abuse that he endured. He unfastened his seatbelt, took a deep breath, put in the gate code (0143), and gained entry into his uncle's community. His uncle met him at the front door and escorted him to the living room.

"You want something to drink?" Brennan asked.

"Nah, I am good," Davis replied.

"So what brings you all the way out here. I must say I was surprised when you called me and told me you were heading over. You acted a little standoffish at Kalila's graduation dinner, and you have been real distant lately. I thought you were mad at me, and that is the last thing I want Davis is you to be mad at me."

"Well, that is why I am here Unc."

"Then you are mad at me?" Brennan asked.

Davis replied, "I didn't come here because I am mad at you, I came cause..."

Brennan interrupted. "Then good, the last thing I want is you to be mad at me nephew. You know that I would do anything for you right?"

Davis reluctantly replied, "Yes I know that Unc."

It was like Davis teleported back in time. He felt like an impressionable nine-year-old boy when he was in his uncle's presence. He found it hard to even look at him in the eyes. His uncle got up out of the seat across from Davis and sat right next to him on the small love seat. Brennan wrapped his arms around Davis and gave him a kiss on the cheek.

Brennan then said, "Whatever I have ever done to you, I want to tell you that I am sorry."

This was Davis's big chance. This was what he came for, to confront his uncle, but he could not utter a single word. He was fighting back tears, and speaking would have caused him to lose it.

"You sure that you don't want nothing to drink?" Brennan asked.

"Nah, I am good. I am going to go, I forgot I was supposed to be helping my dad with this haul," Davis said.

"Next time you have to stay longer, I really miss us spending time together," Brennan said as he led Davis to the front door.

"We have to plan something," Davis said as he exited the door.

"Nephew!" Brennan yelled from the front door as Davis headed to his car.

Davis turned around and said, "Yeah Unc."

Brennan shouted from the front door, "I love you nephew."

Davis replied, "I love you too."

Davis did love his uncle. The strange thing about his love for his uncle was that even though that his uncle hurt him, he couldn't magically make the love that he had for him go away. No matter how much he tried to hate his uncle, he couldn't.

Chapter 32

The End of Love

Kalila & Amanda – May 19, 2004

Kalila sat in the middle of the living room of her almost empty campus apartment wrapping up the few dishes she owned in old newspaper.

"What time is Ren coming to pick up the rest of your things?" Kalila's roommate Amanda said as she exited her bedroom.

"He should be here in about an hour," Kalila responded.

Amanda heard someone blowing their horn downstairs in the parking lot. She looked downstairs, and it was her father.

"Girl, let me get out of here before this man embarrasses me more than he already has. Blowing that circus sounding horn." Amanda said jokingly.

"You better, you remember the last time he started screaming your name out the car's window, " Kalila said as they both laughed.

"Chick, I am going to miss you. You sure you don't want us to drop you off at Ren's dorm?" Amanda asked.

"No girl, I still got a few last minute things to do in this room. You know this school will charge for a sheet of paper left on the floor," Kalila said jokingly.

"Thanks again for letting me have your TV Kay-Kay!"

"No problem, I didn't feel like moving that big ole thing," Kalila replied.

We have been through a lot together. I can't wait until next year. I still can't believe that we both got into the same grad school, look out Tennessee Mountain University, they ain't ready for us," Amanda said as she hugged Kalila goodbye.

Kalila smiled and said, "yeah they don't know what they did."

"You sure you okay Kalila?"

"Yeah girl, just a little tired. Call me when you make it to your parents' house."

172

Kalila hugged Amanda tight and told her that she loved her. In reality, she was not okay, she was broken. She thought that Tristan was the one. The love of her life. The man of her dreams. Tristan helped her to believe that she was worth waiting for. It was in a millisecond everything that she thought that she had was ripped away from her.

She felt an overwhelming hurt that no prayer to her new friend, the "White Jesus" could remedy. She felt as broken as the clock that hung above her in the living room that ran out of batteries two years ago that were never replaced. It has been 3:41pm for a long time now. She felt that her life was out of control, and the little power that she tried to assert was ripped away from her. Every time she thought she was getting ahead, something pulled her back down or tried to stop her. It was like she was running through a glass door. She could see her final destination, but couldn't see the barriers that were in front of her until she ran right into them.

Kalila was sick and tired of being disappointed in love. She yearned for someone to complete her, because deep down inside she felt that she wasn't. Something or someone was missing in her life. Kalila felt that there must be something wrong with her.

Kalila finished wrapping the last box and stacked it neatly in the corner with the other boxes in the now empty apartment. She headed to the bathroom and ran her bath water to take a bath to wash the day away. She dimmed the lights, took off her clothes, pulled out her journal and ripped out one of her poems. She placed the poem on top of the toilet seat. She tested the water with her toe to ensure that it was not too hot, and it was perfect. She submerged her body in the water.

She opened the Tylenol bottle and swallowed a handful of them, and just as she did as a little girl in her Uncle Brennan's pool, she submerged her head in the water. This time she refused to relinquish control, this time she would finally end her love affair with death.

As the air in her lungs began to be replaced with water, she was too drugged to fight.

After knocking for what seemed like an eternity, Ren decided to use his key to open the door to the apartment. When he entered the apartment, he saw the water overflowing from the bathtub seeping out of the bathroom's door. He ran into the bathroom and found Kalila submerge, face down in the tub. Ren removed her naked body from the tub and began CPR.

Ren screamed as he looked down at his sister's lifeless body, "Kalila….. Breathe. Kalila, don't die on me…come on sis fight…fight." As tears flowed from his eyes, he said, "breathe sis, breathe."

Made in the USA
Lexington, KY
21 February 2018